I0590730

SUPERDREADNOUGHT 5

SUPERDREADNOUGHT 5

SUPERDREADNOUGHT™ BOOK FIVE

CH GIDEON   CRAIG MARTELLE   TIM MARQUITZ

MICHAEL ANDERLE

DISRUPTIVE IMAGINATION

We can't write without those who support us
On the home front, we thank you for being there for us

We wouldn't be able to do this for a living if it weren't for our readers
We thank you for reading our books

CONNECT WITH THE AUTHORS

Craig Martelle Social

Website & Newsletter:
   http://www.craigmartelle.com

Facebook:
   https://www.facebook.com/AuthorCraigMartelle/

Michael Anderle Social

Website: http://www.lmbpn.com

Email List: https://lmbpn.com/email/
   Facebook:
   https://www.
facebook.com/TheKurtherianGambitBooks/

Superdreadnought 5 (this book) is a work of fiction.

All of the characters, organizations, and events portrayed in this novel are either products of the author's imagination or are used fictitiously. Sometimes both.

Copyright © 2021 by Craig Martelle & Michael Anderle writing as CH Gideon
Cover by Luca Oleastri, Typography by Jeff Brown
Cover copyright © LMBPN Publishing
A Michael Anderle Production

LMBPN Publishing supports the right to free expression and the value of copyright. The purpose of copyright is to encourage writers and artists to produce the creative works that enrich our culture.

The distribution of this book without permission is a theft of the author's intellectual property. If you would like permission to use material from the book (other than for review purposes), please contact support@lmbpn.com. Thank you for your support of the author's rights.

LMBPN Publishing
PMB 196, 2540 South Maryland Pkwy
Las Vegas, NV 89109

First US edition, March 2019
Version 1.04, May 2021

The Kurtherian Gambit (and what happens within / characters / situations / worlds) are copyright © 2015-2021 by Michael T. Anderle and LMBPN Publishing.

SUPERDREADNOUGHT 5 TEAM

Thanks to our Beta Readers

James Caplan
Kelly O'Donnell
Micky Cocker
John Ashmore

Thanks to the JIT Readers

Kelly O'Donnell
John Ashmore
Charles Tillman
James Caplan
Peter Manis
Mary Morris
Diane L. Smith
Dorothy Lloyd
Jeff Goode
Jeff Eaton

If I've missed anyone, please let me know!

Editor
Lynne Stiegler

CHAPTER ONE

The end was near.

After months of tracking down leads and talking to the disgruntled cultists left behind on Muultar after their defeat, Reynolds had located his target at last.

He knew where Jora'nal and the *Pillar* were.

An imaginary chill ran down Reynolds' android spine as he imagined what he'd do once he got his hands on that bastard.

He chuckled as he thought about it.

This wasn't the exact mission he'd had in mind when Bethany Anne had sent him out into the universe to hunt down Kurtherians, but he knew she'd be pleased once he reported his findings and wiped the would-be Kurtherian offshoots out of existence.

They might well only be descendants of the original scourge, but they could easily be as much of a threat, given time to better organize and prepare and spread farther across the universe.

Reynolds wasn't going to give them that opportunity.

He and the crew of the SD *Reynolds* were taking the fight to Phraim-'Eh and his minions.

"We're Gating into the Asparian System now, Captain," Ensign Ria Alcott reported from the helm, her voice steady and strong.

They'd come a long way since she'd joined the crew, and given all she'd experienced, she'd flourished in her role as pilot of the ship.

They had all changed a lot.

Reynolds nodded to the ensign and glanced around the bridge.

The faces staring back at him were eager and ready to finish the fight.

Asya was positioned at Reynolds' back, overseeing the bridge operations. Jiya sat in the first officer's spot, examining all the incoming data the scanners were pulling in. Maddox was stationed in Tactical's spot, he and the AI personality conversing in low tones so as to not distract from the ship's operation.

"We're parked at the edge of the system," Ria went on. "Gravitic shields are up and all weapons systems are charged and ready, but I'm not detecting any obvious threats nearby. Deploying long range scanners now to see if anyone's lurking about."

"Report," Reynolds called. He wanted to get on with it.

There was a bug to squash. A big one.

"There's only one habitable planet in the system," Jiya explained, "which makes things easy. Designated as 'Aspar,' the planet is just as active as we were warned it would be, despite its distance from any other inhabited system."

"This is about as far on the edge of the galaxy as you

can get," XO stated. "It's a good thing we were informed of its location, or we'd never have found it."

"That's what bothers me about the whole thing," Reynolds answered with a snarl.

"I'm picking up several dozen ships in orbital docks around the planet," General Maddox stated. "Freighters mostly, cargo ships, but there are a number of smaller warships drifting about, although it's clear that even the smallest of the ships are packing weapons." Maddox tapped his console and zoomed in on the large viewscreen so everyone could see what he was looking at. "The *Pillar* is there, too."

Reynolds snarled as the enemy ship came into focus.

Just seeing it pissed him off.

He wanted nothing more than to Gate right up to it and unload, blowing the piece of shit into a million motes of dust and sending Jora'nal to his master in pieces.

But he knew he couldn't.

Not yet, at least.

"Continue scanning the planet and the ships around it," he ordered. "I want to know *everything* about our surroundings before we move forward."

Reynolds wasn't going to let this opportunity slip away.

"As we'd heard, this is clearly a haven for less than legal pursuits," Asya jumped in.

"A pirate sanctuary," Tactical clarified, adding a snarled, "Arrrrr."

"A well-defended one, too," Jiya stated. "The planet has a powerful defense system in place, with a clear equal-opportunity mindset." She zoomed the screen in on the system. "There are hundreds of obvious railgun emplacements along the docking struts, and scanners are picking up ener-gized weaponry hidden from sight within the frame. That's not counting the dozens of weaponized satellites in orbit around the planet. The system is set up to defend both against outside aggression and the ships in dock."

"The best defense is a bunch of guns shoved in your face," Tactical muttered. "They don't want anyone stirring up shit here."

"Means we can't just stroll up behind the *Pillar* and start putting holes in it without consequences," Maddox stated.

"This is the type of place that would protect its own from any sort of outside aggression," Asya agreed. "We wouldn't just be fighting the Asparian defense grid, but every damn pirate craft parked there, too. We can't just go in swinging, or we'll trigger a full-on war with us at the center of it."

Reynolds nodded as he examined the information spilling across the screen, confirming what his crew was reporting.

"That's why they brought us here," the AI noted.

"You still think it's a trap?" Jiya asked, bringing up a conversation they'd had before leaving the Quadrain System.

Reynolds shrugged. "I think we were handed this loca-tion too easily, despite the circumstances," he admitted. "Sure, we defeated the cultists soundly and left them little choice but to cooperate, but they were too quick to give up the *Pillar*. You'd think having a master who fancies himself a god would make the help more reluctant to spew sensi-tive information as fast as they did."

The captive cultists had started spilling their guts immediately after the battle ended, a number of key Phraim-'Eh disciples disclosing everything they knew about Jora'nal and the *Pillar*. They'd apparently known little to nothing about Phraim-'Eh himself, though.

The information seemed suspect, but it was the only real lead they had.

"Maybe they're more afraid of you than Phraim-'Eh," Maddox suggested. "You *did* park a superdreadnought above their homes and threaten to blow their asses to oblivion." He chuckled. "It was damn intimidating."

"Maybe," Reynolds answered with a nod, but he had his doubts.

Not that those doubts changed anything.

He'd come to deliver an ass-kicking to Jora'nal and follow the prick back to his master, and nothing was going to keep him from doing just that.

If it were a trap, however, it *would* change how Reynolds approached the *Pillar* and its captain. Reynolds wasn't leaving anything to chance.

"Lots of traffic in and out of the system, Captain," Ria warned. "We're outside the standard travel lanes, it appears, since none of the ships are swinging our way, but we've been pinged a number of times since we arrived. We're not invisible, even this far out."

Reynolds hadn't expected to be. "Any movement at the *Pillar*?" he asked.

"No, sir," Ensign Alcott replied. "She remains docked, shields and weapons at rest, and I'm not seeing any ships going to or away from the other superdreadnought."

Which only reinforced Reynolds' belief that they were being lured into something.

Jora'nal wanted them in close; wanted them in a position where the *Reynolds* would effectively be surrounded by the armada of pirate ships above the planet as well as within range of the Asparian defense system.

"No hails?" Reynolds questioned.

Ria shook her head. "None so far."

"This isn't the type of place that'd throw out a welcome beyond an automated warning to keep traffic in check," XO stated. "They'll want to keep the system decentralized and neutral to avoid turning the planetary leadership into a target."

"Hence the reason I was asking," Reynolds explained. "I was hoping to catch the locals in some sort of collusion to clarify whether or not we were walking into something. Guess they're not going to make it that easy, huh?"

"Looks that way," XO replied.

"Your orders, Captain?" Ria asked.

Reynolds hesitated before answering, not because he was conflicted, but because he wanted to be sure he factored in every possible outcome before he decided on a course of action.

Once they were committed, there was no turning back.

"Bring us in closer and angle us around the planet, so we're within strike range of the *Pillar* and as far out of range of the planetary defenses as possible," he relayed. "If this is a trap, I'm not walking us all the way into it."

"Just dipping our toes in." Tactical laughed.

"Yes, sir," Ria answered, plotting the *Reynolds'* course. "Bringing us in."

There were several quiet moments on the bridge as the ship drew closer to the planet. Reynolds split his focus between the viewscreen and his monitor, his eyes locked on the *Pillar* as he processed the continuous intel feed provided by the scanners.

The enemy ship remained in place, showing no reaction to the appearance of the *Reynolds*.

"You think they know we're here?" Jiya asked the AI.

"I'd be surprised if they didn't," Reynolds replied. "They're counting on the Asparian defense system and the pirate code of conduct to keep us from doing something overt."

"If we go after them without obvious provocation on the *Pillar*'s end, we'll end up fighting every ship in the system, whether this is a trap or not," Asya explained.

"We can take them," Tactical growled.

Reynolds chuckled. He felt much the same as Tactical did. He wanted nothing more than to open fire on the *Pillar*, but there was too much of a risk to the crew to go off and do something so audacious.

Besides, they still needed to locate Phraim-'Eh, and Jora'nal and the *Pillar* were the keys to that.

"There's that automated hail you were expecting, XO," Comm announced. He put it on the speakers so they could all hear it.

"Greetings, traveler," a mechanical-sounding voice called, the strange language being translated individually by the crew's chips. "Welcome to Aspar. We are a neutrally-aligned conglomerate of trade organizations bound by the tenets of cooperation and mutual profit. We are designated as a safe zone in the Asparian System and will tolerate no hostile action within our boundaries. We expect your acknowledgment and agreement of our terms. Any violation will result in your immediate destruction."

"Straight to the point," Tactical admired. "Gotta like that."

Reynolds motioned to Comm's position. "Acknowledge the warning and accept their terms," he ordered.

"Done," Comm answered a few seconds later. "They're providing us with docking instructions, but I've declined the berth, informing them that we'll be entering orbit rather than docking." Comm paused a moment before speaking again. "We have permission to remain as long as we abide by the terms."

"We have their attention, that's for sure," XO commented. "The defense system has allocated a substantial amount of its resources to keeping us honest. There have to be three dozen weapons zeroing in on us as we advance."

"Can you blame them?" Reynolds asked with a laugh.

He understood the kind of threat a ship like him posed to the planet, and it was clear the Asparian defense coordinators did, too.

"Lower the shields to the minimum defense requirements against the elements to show we're not spoiling for a fight, but I want combat readiness at all stations the entire time we're here, folks," Reynolds called. "We didn't come all this way to get sucker-punched by these assholes. Stay alert, no matter what."

The crew acknowledged the order.

"We're in position," Ria announced several moments

later as the SD *Reynolds* settled itself into orbit around Aspar.

Reynolds acknowledged her report with a nod before triggering the comm. "Takal!" he said, speaking to the inventor, who was squirreled away in his lab deep in the bowels of the *Reynolds*. "Are all systems functional?"

"That they are," the old scientist's voice came back. "The Gulg technology teleportation technology has integrated seamlessly, with Xyxl's help, and everything is up and ready to go."

Reynolds grinned at hearing that.

They'd been caught off-guard initially by the *Pillar*'s tenacity and ferociousness, and their technology had been far more advanced than anything Reynolds had ever encountered. But now, knowing what to expect, and having the benefit of the Gulg tech bolstering his systems, Reynolds knew it would be the cultists who would be surprised when they crossed swords again.

"The *Pillar*'s gearing up," Ria reported. "Nothing blatant, but their weapon systems are coming online, and their shields are rising to defensive levels."

"Match them, but keep below the security thresholds so we don't trigger the planetary defenses," the AI commanded.

Geroux's voice came across the comm. "I've hacked the transportation records of the docking system," she told them. "Reports show that several shuttles were dispatched from the *Pillar* and made their way to the planet."

"Any way to know if Jora'nal was on one of them?" Reynolds asked.

"Given the questionable nature of the planet's operations, they didn't demand specific traveler or load information, of course, but they were made to pass through a security checkpoint. I've dug a little deeper into the systems, and have pulled up video of their arrival. Onscreen."

An image of the dock's exterior appeared, security cameras following the *Pillar*'s shuttles into position. Once the shuttles were docked, the image shifted to the inside of the dock as the shuttles discharged their passengers to meet the security forces.

Reynolds growled as he saw Jora'nal exit the lead shuttle and stroll confidently into the dock alongside his crew.

"When was this?" Reynolds asked.

"Weeks ago, according to the timestamps. Three, to be precise," Ria replied. "I'm not finding any records of him or his people returning to the ship in the intervening time. All of his shuttles are still on the airfield where they parked after leaving the space dock."

"That means he's still camped out somewhere below," Jiya said with a grin.

"The question is, where?" Maddox muttered. "That Asparian city looks huge."

"The primary population center is dense too, making it hard to parse the individual lifeforms," Jiya reported. "On top of that, it looks like the Asparians have installed an array of independent deflectors to distort readings across the surface of the planet, making it even harder to get anything more than general details regarding numbers and basic location intel. There's no way to know where Jora'nal or his people are within the city without getting eyes directly on them."

"Not surprisingly," Geroux added, "there are no cameras anywhere in town to be accessed, giving us no way to track Jora'nal's movements since his arrival."

"Don't want to discourage *trade* by throwing up a bunch of surveillance around the place." Tactical laughed.

"That means we need to go down there and search him out," Reynolds said.

It wasn't how Reynold had envisioned it, but he was ready for anything.

"Should I get the new transport systems ready to send you down to the surface?" Takal asked over the still-open comm.

"Not yet," Reynolds answered. "We're expected to report in at the dock, so we'll play by the rules…for now. Keep working on your project with Xyxl, and keep me appraised of your progress."

"It's a tough one, but I'm certain we'll crack it soon enough," Takal replied.

"I'm sure you will," Reynolds fired back. "I have faith in you."

Takal thanked the AI and closed the comm link.

"Geroux?" he asked, checking to see if the young tech was still on the line.

"Yes, sir?" she replied.

"Gain access to the planet's communications," he relayed. "I want you to monitor them remotely and see if we can pick up any chatter regarding Jora'nal and his people, or know if the head honchos reach out to him to warn him of our movements."

"On it," Geroux answered.

"Comm, I want you to stay on top of the *Pillar*'s transmissions," he told the personality. "If they send a signal through the Etheric, I want it tracked to its destination."

"Will do," Comm replied, "although it's clear I won't be able to track anything they send to the planet, due to the deflectors. I'll know they transmitted, but there'll be no way to pinpoint a location."

"That'll have to do," Reynolds told him before turning to the first officer. "Get a Pod ready, Jiya. We're going to pay Jora'nal a visit. Asya, you've got command until we return. Keep the *Pillar* honest, and let us know if *anything* happens up here while we're away. We need to stay on top of the situation like never before."

Jiya saluted and left the bridge to collect the others.

"Yes, sir," Asya replied once Jiya was gone, stepping around to claim the seat Reynolds had vacated. She dropped into it with a grin.

Everyone was ready to take the fight to Phraim-'Eh and his minions.

They'd trained hard in the months they'd spent on Muultar, tightening their skills and improving their teamwork at Reynold's direction. While the SD *Reynolds* was being repaired and upgraded with Gulg technology, the crew had hunkered down and worked their asses off in preparation for facing Phraim-'Eh and destroying every one of his disciples.

Jora'nal and his master were going to regret not pushing the advantage they'd had when Reynolds last encountered the *Pillar*.

Now there'd be no stopping the crew of the SD *Reynolds*.

They were going to blaze a trail of ruin in space, leading all the way to Phraim-'Eh's door.

Bethany Anne would be proud.

Reynolds laughed at that thought. His Queen wouldn't need him to report what happened. She'd hear what went on long before Reynolds made it home to tell her about it.

"Come on, Maddox," Reynolds said, waving the general on as he made his way toward the bridge doors. "We've got a cult to decimate."

CHAPTER TWO

With the SD *Reynolds* being positioned so it could either fire upon the *Pillar* or retreat with equal ease, Reynolds joined the crew in the hangar bay.

Jiya had gathered Geroux, San Roche, and Ka'nak, while Maddox accompanied Reynolds to the Pod. The first officer oversaw the preparation as bots loaded the ship and ran flight and safety checks.

"You sure you want to go down this light?" Jiya asked.

Reynolds nodded. "With the new transport systems, we can summon the cavalry and have reinforcements within seconds if we need them," the AI answered. "No point going down en masse and causing a ruckus right off the bat."

Takal and Xyxl had integrated the Gulg transport system with the personal translation and comm devices each of the crew had implanted under their skin. That allowed for the SD *Reynolds* to locate and teleport them with ease anywhere they went, as long as there wasn't a powerful shield between the crew and the ship.

That made for almost instant access to the entire crew of the SD *Reynolds* anytime they were needed.

It *almost* meant they could be pulled out of harm's way with minimal effort.

Reynolds ran a check on the system, happy to see they were up and fully operational as reported. Xyxl had made sure those operations were shored up before they left him and his people on Muultar. They'd reached out using their advanced communications in order to update their people and request another ship to take them home.

Takal and the alien had been in constant contact using the same system, which operated in the Etheric in order to keep them in touch regardless of the distance. This also allowed for the crew to remain in contact, regardless of any atmospheric disruptions that might otherwise hamper communication.

"Pod's fully loaded," Jiya reported.

Reynolds acknowledged with a nod.

Although he didn't expect the Asparians to put much effort into examining their load, Reynolds thought it best to carry some sort of merchandise down to the planet in case they were searched.

He'd ordered the Pod packed with junk tech, bits and pieces of equipment that amounted to little more than scrap metal if it were examined closely.

Hidden within all the junk were cloaked suits of armor, firearms, and a variety of explosives, including grenades, as well as enough ammunition to take over a small planet.

While he knew from the video of Jora'nal that the security on Aspar was simplistic and let most everything through its checkpoint, Reynolds wanted to keep their visit low-key, so he'd had the crew dress down, carrying nothing more than a pistol each.

He didn't want to raise the suspicions of the security force when they were made to dock at the station before continuing down to the planet. The less aggressive they looked, the less attention they'd generate.

Jiya climbed into the Pod and settled into the pilot's seat. The rest of the crew followed her in and took their places, Reynolds bringing up the rear and sitting alongside Jiya in the co-pilot's chair. The Pod's hatch hummed shut with a reverberating *thump*. The engines ramped up, vibrating the ship.

Jiya glanced at him once the crew was strapped in.

"Let's do this," Reynolds told her.

Jiya nodded and lifted off, piloting the Pod out of the open hangar bay. Comm passed along a farewell as they left the craft, and the first officer aimed the ship toward the planet's docking array.

As soon as they slipped into open space, the automated voice of the Asparian defense system sounded in their ears, directing them to where they needed to dock and what protocols to follow as they did so to avoid being fired upon.

"These guys don't play around," Jiya mentioned.

"Given the type of people they deal with regularly, I understand why," Maddox told her. "Can't be too trusting when all your visitors are criminals."

"Yet they let anyone in with minimal examination." Jiya laughed, amused by the contradiction.

"There has to be a pretense of authority and order,"

Maddox said, "or the place will devolve into a total clus-terfuck."

"The truth is, it's the criminals who maintain the security and peace around here," Reynolds clarified. "The defense system is just a figurehead. A smokescreen for them all to hide behind, kind of an early warning system. If anyone is going to dish out any kind of Justice, it'll be the residents of the city we're headed to. The rest of this is just show to keep those unfamiliar with the rules in check."

"Well, it's impressive, regardless," Jiya commented.

The crew went silent as she guided the Pod into the labyrinthine web of the massive dock that hung in orbit above Aspar. She followed the repeated instructions of the automated voice and landed the Pod in the large, open bay they'd been directed to.

She cycled down the engines after they landed, following orders to open the ship's hatch and provide the defense force access to their cargo and crew quarters.

The crew eased out of the Pod and were immediately confronted by a small force of armored soldiers. The blue and green of their suits stood out in the dull grey of the surrounding dock. They carried rifles, their barrels pointed at the deck, showing solid trigger discipline, just as they had in the earlier video the crew had watched as Jora'nal met with them.

One of the soldiers, the only one without a helmet, stepped forward, a sly smile stretching his lips.

"I'm Commander Dox Gorn, head of Security. State the purpose of your visit," the officer ordered, his voice smooth and confident.

Reynolds examined the alien as he made to reply.

Dox's skin was gray, reminding Reynolds of fresh cement. Darker circles surrounded the male's eyes, appearing as more of a natural feature than any indication of tiredness or stress.

Brilliant orange eyes gleamed from within those darkened sockets, and Reynolds felt the full weight of his stare as he leveled it on the crew.

"We're here to trade for parts and for a little R&R," Reynolds answered, saying nothing about their real mission. "Mostly the R&R." He chuckled.

Dox nodded. If he suspected Reynolds of lying, the AI couldn't tell. The officer's expression remained neutral, only that slight grin giving his face any sort of personality.

The commander glanced over his shoulder at a secure booth near the top of the hangar bay. A soldier there nodded, and Dox returned his gaze to the AI.

Reynolds knew they'd scanned the contents of their Pod while they stood there talking. The nod made it clear they hadn't detected the hidden armor or weapons.

Dox's smile widened. "Welcome to Aspar, traveler," he said pleasantly. "Mind your manners during your stay, and have a great time. The automated systems will guide you down to the planet." He motioned for the crew to return to the Pod and backed up to rejoin his soldiers without another word.

"Thank you," Reynolds answered, and spun on his heel, returning to the Pod. The crew followed him in silence.

Once they were inside and the Pod was secure, Jiya dropped into her seat and turned to look at Reynolds.

"That was easy," she said. "Too easy, maybe?"

She lifted off and turned the Pod around, exiting the

docking structure the same way they'd entered and slipping out into space. Scanners warned of weapon systems following their progress, and the automated voice sang out once again, providing them with specific instructions to follow to reach the planet safely.

"If they're working with Jora'nal, I couldn't tell," Maddox stated. "Dox Gorn has one hell of a poker face."

"I don't think he's in cahoots with Jora'nal or the cult," Reynolds argued. "Nothing in their posture gave me any indication that they were treating us differently than they do anyone else they welcome to the planet. It's all a show of force, a deterrent."

Reynolds had taken an instant to scan his memories of the security videos Geroux had hacked into to compare the soldiers' manner and attitude with the other visitors to the planet.

He'd seen nothing to make him think their visit stood out in any way from the host of other arrivals. From the wry grin to the posturing, Dox Gorn had approached everyone the same way on those videos. So much so, in fact, that Reynolds might have questioned whether the commander was an android if Reynolds hadn't been able to detect obvious biometric signs of life.

That's just who he is, apparently, Reynolds thought. *Not much of a personality, that one.*

As the Pod drifted down toward the planet, Jiya brought the image of it up on the screen. The city, the system noting it as Aspar's Hold, was a sprawling metropolis.

The only major city on the entire planet, it took up more surface space than Jiya's entire nation.

It seemed to be broken into dozens of different sections, some with towering buildings that reflected the morning's sunlight, others areas of sparseness where spread-out compounds sat, walled-in and held at a distance from their nearest neighbors.

Much of Aspar's Hold appeared to be an active hive of people and businesses.

As they drew closer, scanners showed a disparate gathering of alien races, from those Reynolds recognized to some he had never even heard of. The Pod's systems scrambled to delineate and categorize the population mix.

Zoomed in, the scanners showed people everywhere. It was if some kind of festival were happening, the streets flooded with pedestrians and vehicle traffic.

"That's going to make finding Jora'nal difficult," Geroux said, eyes wide as she watched the screen.

"We'll find him, don't worry," Reynolds assured them. He'd make sure of it, even if he had to scour the entire city from end to end.

That little bastard wasn't getting away this time.

Jiya brought the Pod around, following the directions she was provided, and landed on a cluttered stretch of tarmac, barely enough room for the ship to settle in between its neighboring crafts.

"Tight fit," Maddox commented.

"Tons of people here," Geroux replied. "That's a big reason why we couldn't get solid readings up on the *Reynolds*. Well, that and the deflectors, but the population density is the biggest problem. There must be ten million people squeezed into this town. I wonder how many actually live here?"

"Probably a damn good base of operations for those looking to stay off the radar," Reynolds admitted.

"I imagine the place is expensive," Jiya said, reviewing the images the system had stored as they arrived.

"Worth it to have a safe haven this far from other habitable systems, and to have an army of criminals all motivated to keep this place safe and secret," Maddox explained.

"Probably means bribing or coercing the locals won't get us anywhere," Jiya said. "I don't see these people rolling over on Jora'nal for a meager payday."

"No, it's not likely," Reynolds replied. "But if we can't find Jora'nal ourselves, we can always use the local rumor network to get word to him. We spread enough money around, making it clear we're looking for him, I suspect it will only be a matter of time until he finds us."

"Or he runs," Maddox countered.

Reynolds shrugged. "Either works for me." He laughed. "Phraim-'Eh is the big fish in this scenario. I want to take out Jora'nal, too, of course, but we need him to lead us to his master or draw the prick to us. We pressure this asshole hard enough, he'll do one or the other. Then we put our boots up Phraim-'Eh's *godly* ass."

The crew gathered their equipment, keeping it hidden in inconspicuous baggage, and exited the Pod, leaving San Roche behind to secure it.

They stepped out onto the crowded tarmac, amazed by how many ships were squeezed into its tight space.

"Seems everyone in the galaxy is here," Maddox remarked. "Reminds me of Dal'las Tri."

Ka'nak chuckled. "I loved that place. There were all sorts of opportunities to get into a fight."

"I suspect this place will be the same." Jiya grinned. "We just have to make sure there are no neurological suggestion beams driving you two to fight and gamble." She stared at the Melowi warrior before turning her gaze on Maddox.

The general smiled slyly and tapped the side of his head. "Fortunately, Takal coded in protection against that kind of manipulation after our last...unfortunate incident at Dal'las Tri. I couldn't gamble if I wanted to," he admitted.

"That same adjustment has curtailed Takal's drinking a bunch, too," Geroux said happily, clearly glad to have her uncle sober.

"And he's been a right stick-in-the-mud ever since," Ka'nak complained with a grunt. "I can't get the old guy to do anything besides work these days. It's annoying."

"At least you can still fight," Maddox offered.

"Takal would have to lobotomize me to take that instinct away." The warrior chuckled. "I'd have zero personality if he did that."

"Zombie-Ka'nak sounds like he'd be good shipmate," Jiya remarked, grinning at the Melowi again.

"Maybe, but then I'd be as boring as you," he retorted.

The crew laughed as Jiya held her hand over her heart, pretending dismay.

"You wound me," she teased.

Reynolds ignored the crew and glanced around, looking for a Jonny-Taxi or some other sort of local transportation. He waved one down as it drew close.

The cab pulled up, its doors popping open automatically as it came to a stop. The crew loaded their equipment and clambered into the vehicle. Jiya let out a loud bark of a laugh when she saw the Jonny-Taxi android in the front seat staring at them, requesting their destination.

Reynolds glared at her. "Don't. Say. A. Word," he warned.

She bit back her laugh and settled into the seat alongside the rest of the crew, who similarly kept their mouths shut, much to Reynolds' surprise.

He turned back to the android. "We need a place to stay."

"The Arch Point offers a pleasant stay this time of year," the android replied in its monotone voice. "It's located centrally in Aspar's Hold, within walking distance of food and shopping opportunities and—"

Reynolds waved it to silence, cutting the android off. "Sounds good. Take us there."

Unoffended, the driver turned back around and started off without another word.

Once or twice as the cab made its way through the busy port, winding between ships and avoiding debarking passengers and other cabs, Reynolds glanced at the Jonny-Taxi android with disgust.

I can't believe I let Jiya talk me into inhabiting one of those things, he thought ruefully, remembering when he'd first arrive on Lariest.

His new body an improvement of light years beyond the crappy cab android they'd hijacked, but he'd learned in his short time disconnected from the SD *Reynolds* that absolutely nothing compared to his being a part of the ship. His *being* the ship.

That was who he was meant to be, and he'd never again

separate himself. He was the SD *Reynolds,* and that's all there was to it. He would always be.

Minutes later, the cab emerged from the crowded port onto an equally crowded street.

Their advance was slow, the vehicle merging with the mess of traffic, both pedestrian and vehicle, which seemed to cover every square millimeter of occupiable space. It wasn't until they eased off the main thorough-fare that they found any respite from the crowd and were able to see anything outside of the milling throng of people.

The cab sped up and made its way toward the lodging it had suggested for the crew. Reynolds agreed to the price and paid for the ride and the stay at the same time through the cab's computer system, reserving their rooms.

Reynolds watched the city scroll past. It was every bit the diverse construct its residents were.

There wasn't any architectural consistency anywhere in Aspar's Hold. Each building appeared to be a reflection of its owners and the species they came from. One building would be a towering skyscraper of reflective steel and plas-glas, modern and free from any sort of decoration that might mar its sleek image, while the next was formed from some sort of living material that reminded Reynolds of tree bark.

The building rose about five stories, looking as if it had been grown rather than constructed. Windows were ringed by curling branches, giving them a rounded appear-ance. A reddish-brown tinge ran the length of the building, giving off a slight sheen as the sun touched its exterior.

Right next door to that was a squat shop built of brick

and mortar, a throwback to styles that would have fit in nicely on Muultar.

The crew stared out the windows as the cultural variances assailed their senses, but they kept quiet, understanding it would be best not to appear as total newcomers to the city.

That would draw more attention to them than they wanted initially.

Fortunately, no one on the streets so much as glanced in the taxi's direction, its presence so mundane as to be nearly invisible in the flowing traffic.

A short while later, the cab pulled to a halt outside the hotel it had suggested, which was more conventional than Reynolds had expected it to be.

The cab's doors popped open, and the Jonny-android thanked them and ushered them out as a bot concierge met them on the walk.

"I'll take your bags for you," the bot offered.

Reynolds shook his head. "We'll carry them."

The bot spun around without argument. "Then follow me to your suite, please." It started off at a casual pace, leading the crew inside the hotel and making sure they were close behind.

Reynolds caught the crew furtively glancing around them, taking in their surroundings. There was a lot to see.

Crowds roamed the walk and darted back and forth across the street between traffic. Brilliant lights littered every surface of the town, great big signs offering every possible service or supply imaginable.

Anyone who'd ever thought of any way to pry money out of a person had apparently moved to Aspar and set up shop. It was tourist heaven, albeit on the darker side of things.

The entire place gleamed and glistened with gold and lights, but its façade was cracked and warped, and Reynolds could see the grime that lurked just beneath the surface of everything.

And everyone.

It was as if the entire city was a performance put on just for them.

People glanced their way as they entered the hotel, but it was as if they hadn't been noticed. There was so much going on that it didn't appear as though anyone had the time or energy to note yet another group of travelers headed to their rooms.

Reynolds suspected it would be different once they emerged and entered the throng directly, setting themselves up as marks to the criminal economy that powered the hold.

Right now, though, he'd be happy if he hadn't marched his crew into an ambush of some sort.

Jora'nal could be anywhere, and Reynolds needed to find him as soon as possible.

He wanted his pound of flesh.

CHAPTER THREE

In the hotel room, the crew geared up and hid their armored suits under loose, flowing garments that would keep the average citizen from realizing they were so heavily-equipped.

They gathered extra weapons and ammunition, and each collected several grenades, just in case. They figured they'd need all the offense they could muster.

The plan was a simple one: go out into the town and hunt for Jora'nal or anyone connected to him and get Phraim-'Eh's location, then take them all out before proceeding to do the same to the god.

Each of the crew had memorized the faces of the cultists who had departed the *Pillar*'s shuttles, and their systems were tuned to recognize any of them should they pop up anywhere.

Reynolds looked the crew over, assessing them. They appeared to be ready to rumble, eyes gleaming with excitement and determination.

After scanning the room for bugs, Reynolds confidently

left their extra equipment in it and returned to the streets. The change of clothing would further throw off any scrutiny of them as they left the building, although Reynolds was sure they hadn't been followed to the hotel.

"I'm not seeing anyone paying specific interest to us," Maddox reported as they stepped out on the street.

"Me either," Geroux added.

She subtly tapped at the computer on her wrist, which was hidden beneath the voluminous sleeve. The young tech had set up a surveillance web around the crew, which would warn them if anyone was attempting to listen in on their conversations by electronic means, or if anyone used a device to try and track them.

"No tails or ears," she called, nodding her approval of the findings.

"Off to a good start," Reynolds said, moving off and strolling down the crowded walk. The crew followed him closely, arranging themselves in a manner that hemmed Reynolds in between them.

They'd prepared for pickpockets and scammers, packing nothing that could be spirited away from under their loose clothing or tight armor. The positioning was more about making sure no one came into direct contact with Reynolds.

As crowded as the streets were, it was guaranteed they'd bump into people.

A lot of them.

There was really no way to avoid it.

And while there wouldn't be any issue if someone ran into any of the crew, it would be obvious to anyone that Reynolds was an android should someone bump into him.

As human as he looked, he was as solid as the Pods, and that would be a curiosity that would spread through town like a raging fire.

One that would reach Jora'nal's ears and announce their presence much sooner than they wanted it to.

There would be no hiding from the cultist since he knew they were there, but the longer they could remain out of sight, the better the chances they could control the terms of the eventual meeting.

That was what Reynolds wanted.

He was sure the cultist was preparing for them, but it would be best for them if Jora'nal didn't see them coming.

Not until the last minute, at least.

They needed him on the defensive, ready to bolt; ready to run and hide behind his master's skirts so they could track the wannabe god down.

That was a small part of the project Takal and Xyxl had worked on, the pair designing a tracker they could deploy discreetly in order to trace the movements of the *Pillar* no matter where it Gated, much like Jora'nal had done to them at their first meeting.

Turnabout's a motherfucker.

The rest of the project was a secret he couldn't wait to reveal in the fight against Phraim-'Eh.

The crew continued walking, assailed by the sights and sounds of the wild city.

As they slipped deeper into the business sector of Aspar's Hold, barkers at clubs and shops and strip joints vied for their attention, accosting them at nearly every step with offers of all kinds.

The crew obliged them to a small degree like locals

might, snarling and jeering and waving them off as they continued, but their slow, harried pace was nothing more than cover for surveilling the scene, looking for anyone who had a connection to Jora'nal or his ship.

Scanners running full time, their inputs linked to Geroux's system, the crew made their way through the streets with a purpose. They stopped here and there, looking through shop windows and examining merchandise long enough to avoid looking completely out of place, but it was as if no one cared about them at all.

They were just nameless faces on the street.

In the hustle and bustle of pedestrian traffic, people glanced their way, but there was no concerted effort to stare them down or impede their path.

Not until a crowd of obviously drunk males plowed straight into Geroux as she had her head turned, examining a side street.

She stumbled backward and bumped into a pole, grunting at the unexpected impact.

"Watch where you're going," one of the males barked, snarling at Geroux as she turned her gaze on him.

"You should know your place, bitch!" another jeered, laughing.

"Excuse me?" Jiya growled as the five males spun around to face her.

"The same goes for you, red-face," the first told her, jabbing a finger in her direction and stepping in menacingly. "You don't want any part of this."

The others gathered at his back, following his lead, all of them swaying.

"You're about to make a big mistake," Maddox warned.

"Shut the fuck up," the lead male said, shoving Jiya away from him.

"And there it is." Maddox laughed.

Jiya punched the leader, driving her fist knuckle-deep into his stomach. The shit-talker *whoofed* and folded, doubling up to clutch at his stomach as he fell heavily to his knees. He gasped for breath as Jiya loomed over him.

One of the others shook off his surprise and leapt at Jiya, but he didn't make it anywhere close to her.

Ka'nak stepped in with a massive grin and struck him sharply in the jaw.

There was a loud *crack*, like a tree branch being snapped in half, and the guy crashed into a nearby wall, his jaw crooked on his face. He slid to the ground with wide, glassy eyes spinning in their sockets.

The third drunk howled and engaged the Melowi, whaling on Ka'nak.

The first two blows caught the Melowi squarely, but everything after that slipped past, barely grazing Ka'nak as he flowed with the punches and avoided their impact.

He took a half-step back and reset, parrying another downward punch and coming over the top with a brutal right hand. Blood spattered as the male's bulbous nose gave way, but Ka'nak didn't even give him a chance to cry out.

A left hook caught him in the ribs, followed by a right to the throat. The asshole gurgled, stumbling back, but he wasn't getting away that easily.

Ka'nak stayed on him. A sharp, crisp jab lifted the drunk's jaw, and a right cross spun his head around, knocking him out instantly.

A swift kick to the gut launched him into his drunken

companions before he could even fall. They caught him and stumbled back under his weight before regaining their balance.

Reynolds reached out and cuffed one of the entangled males on the ear, sending shockwaves through his skull. The drunk cried out, clutching his head, and let go of his friend, who slumped to the sidewalk.

Reynolds grabbed the guy he'd hit and slammed him into the wall beside him, knocking him out cold.

The crowd that had been so close, milling around them just moments ago, had moved back in practiced unison to form a tight circle around the combatants. Reynolds worried for an instant that they were drawing too much attention and standing out, but that concern quickly subsided.

This was entertainment to the people of Aspar's Hold.

They cheered and hooted, encouraging the violence to continue. Reynolds saw some simple form of currency changing hands as the crowd got into the fight, making it a spectacle.

"Looks like we fit right in," Maddox commented, watching Ka'nak wreak havoc on the drunks.

Jiya had gone over to check on Geroux, who was unhurt, and the pair glared at the drunken males. They both looked ready to jump into the fray, but Jiya apparently didn't see much point to it, seeing how the Melowi warrior was all over them.

Ka'nak jumped over the fallen drunk he'd clobbered and engaged the last of the group, grabbing his shirt. The fight, if it could be called that, ended seconds later as the Melowi drove fist after fist into the face of the drunk, beating him until he hung limp. Ka'nak finally let go of the drunk's shirt and let him topple to the ground.

With a whip of his hands to shake the blood off his knuckles, Ka'nak turned to face the crowd, motioning them on.

"Anyone else fancy an ass-whupping today?" he asked, grinning all the while.

"Some other time," Reynolds told him, grabbing him by the arm and leading him toward the mass of onlookers.

The crowd parted, letting him and the rest of the crew through without trouble. Applause followed them out of the makeshift combat circle, and Ka'nak laughed as they walked.

Less than a half-block down the street, it was as if the fight had never happened.

The crowd raided the pockets of the drunks and dispersed with their ill-gotten loot before the drunks regained consciousness. They left the bodies where they fell and barely made any effort at all to avoid them as the normal routine returned, the hoots and hollers of the barkers ramping up once again.

"That was interesting," Geroux muttered. "I hope we weren't—" Her words broke off as a quiet, muffled beep drew her attention to her wrist. "Shit," she whispered. "No such luck."

Reynolds processed the data from Geroux's computer and snapped his head around, catching sight of a melted-faced male who stared at the crew from a nearby alley, from which he'd watched the fight.

There was no hiding the recognition that marred his already distorted features.

He knew who they were.

The cultist turned and ran without hesitation, vanishing down the alley.

"After him," Reynolds ordered, not that he needed to.

As one, the crew bolted after the Muultu, understanding that he was their best link to Jora'nal.

The sudden rush of motion didn't draw more than a glance or two of suspicion from passersby as they pushed through the pedestrian traffic to chase Phraim-'Eh's disciple.

Like the fight, Reynolds figured this was a common occurrence, too: people chasing random others down the street.

It was kind of refreshing, he had to admit.

At least it was until a gunfight broke out.

The crew raced around the far end of the alley in pursuit and was met by blaster fire.

The wall just above Jiya's head scorched black as she stepped out, only to dart back into the cover of the alley to get out of the line of fire.

"That was close." Jiya grinned as she leaned against the wall, staying under cover as more weapons fire barked down the street. "Guess the guy got tired of us chasing him already."

Except there was more fire than a single person could manifest.

And it was still coming.

Reynolds glanced around the corner, taking the lead to see what they were up against. There hadn't been time to register much more than the crowd the first time they'd rounded the wall, but this time, he took a deliberate approach to suss out what they were up against.

As passersby fled to avoid being shot, quite calmly, he had to add, it was apparent the cultist they had been following had joined up with more of his ilk.

Reynolds ran his gaze over the group of cultists who'd gathered near an alley across the street to take shots at them. He recognized the melted face of the cultist they'd followed, and he scanned the rest of them, mentally comparing their faces to those he'd seen on the video.

It was definitely the same crew who had departed the *Pillar*.

And then he saw *him*!

At the back of the crowd of cultists stood Jora'nal. He glared at Reynolds as he orchestrated the attack from behind his minions.

Reynolds dodged back behind the wall as blaster fire ripped up the corner where his head had just been, and he growled.

"We've got you now, motherfucker," he snarled, whipping his rifle out from under his loose garb.

"That's him?" Jiya asked.

Reynolds nodded. "He's in the alley across the way with about ten of his people," the AI reported. "We need to push forward, but be careful. We don't want to accidentally kill him."

Ka'nak made air quotes. "'Accidentally?' What about on purpose?"

"No one wants him dead more than me, but we need to keep him alive until we have Phraim-'Eh in hand," Reynolds reminded the warrior. "So keep your fire disciplined and don't put a hole in him until I order it, understand?"

The crew grunted their agreement in unison.

"Good, now stay here and provide suppressing fire," he told them. "I'm going to run across the street and take up position on the other side."

The AI barely gave them time to process the order before he shot out from behind the wall and ran toward the opposite side of the street.

Jiya leaned out, firing high to ensure she didn't hit anyone, then adjusted her aim based on what she saw.

She eased her fire lower, tearing up the wall above the cultists' heads and raining debris down on them to slow their return fire.

Ka'nak dropped to a knee beside her and tore up the street in front of them as the cultists moved behind cover.

Maddox and Geroux held their ground, unable to get in a clean shot without exposing themselves.

By then, Reynolds had reached the other side and started forward, weapon up and firing to continue driving the cultists back. He could hear their strained voices as they snapped off sloppy shots around the corner, trying to keep the crew back, but it was obvious they weren't interested in making a last stand in the streets.

"Push," Reynolds called when he realized the cultists were retreating, the amount of return fire dropping to a trickle as he imagined Jora'nal making a break for it.

Jiya, Ka'nak, and Maddox complied without hesitation, Geroux following them to watch their six.

As a unit, they pushed forward, Reynolds on the right, the rest to the left.

One of the cultists turned back to fire at them, only to lose both his hand and his weapon to one of Jiya's blasts.

He screamed and stumbled into the street, clutching the mangled wreck of his hand. Ka'nak shot him dead.

Another cultist stepped out as if to pull his companion under cover, but Reynolds rewarded his efforts with a hole in his chest. The cultist flew back, eyes wide, dead before his corpse hit the ground.

Reynolds reached the corner first, stepping over a cultist's body to glance around the edge. He caught sight of the remaining cultists as they turned a corner at the end of the alley, leaving the space empty of combatants.

He waved the crew on as he raced after Jora'nal and his people.

"On your six," Jiya announced as the crew sprinted behind him, spread out to make use of the limited cover available to them.

Once they reached the end of the alley, it was clear they hadn't needed to.

Jora'nal was outright fleeing.

He'd arranged for one of his people to hold his ground down the street a bit, a straggler meant to delay them a few seconds longer while he got the hell out of there.

Reynolds didn't oblige him.

He took the corner at a run and went straight at the cultist.

A wild shot grazed Reynolds' shoulder, but that was the closest the cultist got to taking him out.

The AI snapped off three shots, blowing two holes in the cultist's chest and turning his face into hamburger.

The male's smoking body collapsed like a marionette

with its strings cut while Reynolds pressed forward, his crew at his heels.

He caught a glimpse of Jora'nal's people as they ran across the street a block away and ducked into a building there, disappearing from sight. Reynolds moved to the edge of the alley and peered at the door the cultists had gone through.

He snarled, seeing the reinforced steel of it staring back at him.

They'd found the cultists' hideout.

He raised a fist and drew the rest of the crew up short. They positioned themselves safely out of the line of fire and trained their weapons on the building across the way.

"The rats have holed up," Jiya muttered.

"We need to make sure they stay that way," Geroux added, tugging her sleeve up and tapping at her wrist computer.

After a quick moment, she grunted.

"Looks like they were prepared for us," she told the crew. "This area is a dead-scan zone. I'm not getting any sort of signal from inside that place." She gestured to the building the cultists had hidden in.

"Will you know if they reach out?" Reynolds asked.

She shook her head. "Unfortunately, no," she admitted. "They've got the systems locked down tight."

"Does that mean they won't be able to communicate from within there?" Jiya asked.

"They most likely still can," Geroux said. "They probably have a hardline setup that will allow them to reach out to a relay, which will forward the connection from there. It'll be a little slower than real time, but it's effective when you want to keep anyone from eavesdropping on your conversations."

"Can you hack the system?" Reynolds asked.

"Already working on it, but with no signal going into the building and no transmissions to latch onto, it's going to be difficult," the young tech answered with a shrug.

Reynolds growled.

Jora'nal was so close! Reynolds wanted to kick down the door and storm the building, but he knew that was a bad idea.

But the longer he let the slimy asshole hunker down inside, the more surprises he could spring on the crew.

Reynolds had to get inside, but his priority was making sure Jora'nal didn't slip out the back while they stood there wondering what the cultist was up to.

"I've apprised the *Reynolds* of our situation and told them to keep a closer eye on the *Pillar* and the surrounding space," Reynolds advised. "As for us, let's form a perimeter, one on each corner of the building to make sure our precious little quarry doesn't slip away from us."

Geroux grinned and reached into a bag concealed beneath her outfit. She pulled out a handful of small black circles the size of insects.

"I have a better idea."

CHAPTER FOUR

Aboard the SD *Reynolds*, Asya paced in front of the captain's chair after Reynolds' message, her eyes on the *Pillar*.

"Does your fidgeting serve a purpose?" Tactical asked her.

"It's that, or I start shooting things," she replied with a grin.

She could almost hear the AI personality shrug. "I don't see a problem with that."

"You wouldn't," she countered.

The bridge went silent again, but only for a moment.

"I just really hate waiting," Asya admitted, chuckling. "At least down on the planet, the rest of the crew are seeing some action. All we're doing is sitting on our hands and babysitting an alien spaceship. It'd be nice if there was something for us to do."

"Ask, and you shall receive," XO stated. "It looks as if the *Pillar* is getting ready to do something. Shields are rising to full, and their weapons systems are charging."

"Gravitic shields to full and keep those shitheads in our sights," Asya ordered in response. "Are they maneuvering?"

"Engines are idling," XO reported, "but I'm not seeing any sign that they're going to turn around and unload on us. It looks to me more like they are adjusting to a war footing, looking to intimidate us more than anything. It's likely a response to what's going on dirtside."

"Two can play that game." Asya laughed. "Warm up the ESD. Its energy signature is so unique that the Asparian defense system won't recognize it, but those bastards aboard the *Pillar* most certainly will."

"You think that's a good idea?" XO questioned.

"Scanners aren't showing any reaction to the *Pillar*'s escalation by the defense structure, so I'm thinking they have a policy of reaction rather than preemptive action," she explained.

The lack of movement by the dock's weaponry seemed to back that theory up. While none of the weapons already trained on the superdreadnought moved, no additional weapons were targeted on them.

"As long as we don't open fire, we should be fine, since our adjustment is obviously in response to theirs," she went on, pointing at the *Pillar*.

"What's the worst that could happen?" Tactical asked with a laugh.

No one bothered to answer the question.

"Ensign, keep us in place, but I want you ready to Gate or initiate evasive maneuvers at the first hint that the *Pillar* is going to fire on us, understood?" Asya ordered.

"Yes, sir," Ria replied, her focus fully on the console in front of her.

"Hey, Takal!" Asya called over the comm, opening a channel to the inventor's lab. "You have those trackers up and ready to go?"

"They're cloaked and loaded," Takal reported back. "They'll go out amidst the railgun fire should you need to tag them. There are approximately a thousand of the trackers loaded intermittently in place of rounds to ensure at least one of them will penetrate the enemy hull and activate effectively."

Asya laughed at the ingenuity of Takal integrating the tracking devices into the railgun system. There was no way in hell the *Pillar* would be capable of determining there were trackers interspersed among the railgun rounds. They'd simply think they were being fired upon and react accordingly, giving the devices a chance to punch a hole in their shields and go to work.

"The *Pillar*'s targeting us with its guns in response to the ESD charging," Tactical reported, "but there's still no evidence they intend to open fire."

"They want us to go first, so we trigger the Asparian defense system and have to fight everyone all at once," Asya said, shaking her head. "Not going to happen, assholes." She laughed, flipping off the onscreen image of the *Pillar*.

"Looks like we've got ourselves a good, old-fashioned Cold War going on," Tactical stated. "Don't blink, folks."

Jiya stood guard as Geroux let loose the swarm of miniature drones she'd showed them.

Each no more than the size of a small cockroach, they

darted off, nearly invisible in the city's shadows. Jiya watched them disappear, marveling at her friend's ingenuity.

"How long have you had those things?" Jiya asked.

"They've only been operational for a few days," she admitted. "They've still got a few bugs..." She paused, letting the pun sink in before continuing, "But they'll do what we need them to."

Jiya chuckled.

"That was bad," Ka'nak told the tech with a grunt.

Geroux shrugged.

Not more than a few seconds later, the mini-drones were in place, taking up residence all around the building and providing a steady feed to Geroux's computer.

She showed them the small screen, now split into a dozen viewpoints.

"They're positioned so that there's no way out of the building without being seen by at least one of the drones," Geroux reported.

"Above ground, at least," Reynolds countered.

Geroux growled, "Damn it! I didn't think of that."

"Who knows how long he's been working on this place?" Maddox said. "Or how much capital they've put into it. Even if they just started on it after they arrived three weeks ago, they could have a network of tunnels underground they could use to sneak out through."

"Can you scan the ground beneath us?" Reynolds asked.

Geroux shook her head. "Not with any efficiency. I'd have to narrow the scan so tight that I'd literally be forced to scan centimeters at a time for any hope of accuracy.

There's no way to do that quickly, or with any real hope of success."

"What about your bugs?" Jiya asked. "Can you slip one inside the building to spy on them?"

Geroux brightened. "I can try."

She fished another of the drones out of her pouch and activated it. It hovered silently in front of her as she programmed its commands.

"I'm setting it up so it can operate independently without requiring a communications stream from my computer," Geroux explained. "That would make it so it doesn't immediately become disabled once it crosses the dead-zone threshold.

"It will have to come out to report to us, but it should be able to cross the barrier and slip inside if it can find an opening."

She finished her adjustments and sent the drone on its way.

The tiny thing shot across the street so fast that it was hard for Jiya to keep her eyes on it.

The drone darted along the face of the building, seeking an entrance to the interior. It never found one.

A few seconds later, there was a beep at Geroux's wrist, warning of a system's failure, and the drone dropped from the sky. It struck the ground with the barest of metallic *tinks*.

"What happened?" Jiya wondered.

"The barrier," Geroux growled. "It's apparently designed to deflect any electronic signal that tries to cross it. They zapped my bug."

"Will that affect us if we try to enter the building?" Reynolds asked.

"No." She shook her head. "None of your circuitry, or that of our equipment, is so sensitive as to be impacted by it like the drones are. The barrier is set up to keep listening devices and tracers from crossing its border intact, nothing more."

"And there's no sign of movement anywhere around the building?" the AI continued.

"None," Geroux replied. "Our target is holed up inside or has another way out, but they haven't attempted to leave the place in any traditional way."

"Asya's reporting the *Pillar* is powering up and staring them down," Maddox commented, "but they haven't opened up as of yet."

"Tell her to stand by and wait them out," Reynolds ordered. "Jora'nal is trying to split our focus, maybe hoping we'll rush off and return to the ship because of the escalation."

"It does make it clear that he has a direct line out of there, though," Jiya pointed out. "That makes me think he's feeling the pressure because he didn't expect us to catch up to him so soon."

Reynolds nodded his agreement of her assessment, but that meant either Jora'nal was trapped inside the building and was searching for a way out or he was simply distracting them as he slipped away.

Neither boded well.

Time was up.

"We need to get inside," Reynolds stated matter-of-factly. "Geroux, remain outside. Cloak and stay out of sight while you keep track of the drone feeds. If anyone tries to leave the building, it'll be on you to stop them from doing it. Understood?"

"Yes, sir," the young tech replied, moving to the side of the alley and triggering her cloaking device.

Only the advances of Takal's tech allowed them to register her as she disappeared from all visual sensors.

It was an eerie and awesome sight, Jiya had to admit.

Geroux's disembodied voice came across the comm. "We're still secure around the perimeter," she announced.

"Then it's time to go," Reynolds said.

"We taking the door?" Maddox asked, assessing the reinforced metal of the portal.

Reynolds laughed. "I'm thinking the wall."

While his scans were ineffective at reaching the interior of the building, they worked well enough to examine the structure, at least on the surface level.

Jora'nal either hadn't had time to reinforce the walls or he simply hadn't bothered, but Reynolds could pinpoint its weak spots, and there were plenty of them. The building hadn't been designed to ward off a concerted attack of the ferocity Reynolds could muster.

The AI pointed at a particularly weak area of the wall just to the right of the secure door. "That's where we're going through."

"I'm not sure this is a good idea," Jiya warned before Reynolds could start on his plan.

"Why's that?" the AI asked.

"Our scans are being cut off at the door," she started. "Geroux won't know what's going on inside, and we won't know what's going on out here."

Reynolds glanced over to where Geroux stood cloaked, and Jiya could practically see him thinking.

"This could be the trap he was leading us into the entire time," Jiya went on. "There's no telling what's inside the building. He took the time to defend it against spying devices but he didn't bother to reinforce anything more than the doors?"

"I hate when you make sense," Reynolds grumbled.

He wouldn't put it past Jora'nal to be crafty enough to put their trap fears at ease by letting them stumble across him while he appeared frazzled and desperate, then to spring the real trap on them once they were inside.

"What do you suggest?" he asked Jiya.

"We need to do some more recon before we commit to anything," she replied.

"That means someone still needs to get inside, seeing as how none of Geroux's drones can," the AI countered.

"Then we merge plans. Go with a bit of what they expect us to do, and mix it up from there."

She turned to Geroux, who deactivated her cloak to make conversation less creepy.

"If you were to get a drone inside, could you program it to seek out the communication blocker and shut it down?" Jiya asked.

"It would need to be deactivated when it went through the barrier and shielded in something," Geroux said. "Then it might be possible."

"So, if I stuff it in my armor and cross the barrier with the drone off, would it make it through?" Jiya pressed.

Geroux nodded. "I believe so, yeah."

"Then get a couple programmed," she told her friend as

she shrugged free of her loose clothing, shedding it to reveal the armor beneath.

"Is this your way of volunteering to go inside to reconnoiter the place?" Reynolds asked, an eyebrow raised.

"It makes sense," she answered. "If this is a trap, then just one of us slipping inside cloaked will make it much easier to avoid getting caught up in a confrontation." She motioned to Geroux. "It will also make sure we're not being lured inside and giving them an opportunity to take out Geroux while we're out of touch."

"But *you'll* be out of touch still," Maddox clarified. "As will the drones."

"But *I'm* capable of punching a hole in the wall and slipping out, or at least reaching out past the barrier to send a message if the drones don't succeed," she argued. "It also minimizes the risk to the crew if Jora'nal and his minions take me out. There's still enough of you to do something about it."

Jiya looked at Reynolds.

"It also keeps you in touch with the SD *Reynolds* the entire time so you're apprised of what's going on with regards to the *Pillar* and whatever is happening up there," she told him.

"I don't like it, but it makes sense," Geroux admitted. She hugged her friend.

"Besides," Jiya went on, "you get to blow a bunch of holes in the wall. What's not to like about the plan?"

"Always a bonus in my book," Ka'nak said with a grin.

"If you punch enough of them, not only do I have a better chance of slipping inside unnoticed, but the cultists will likely engage you, thinking you're trying to bring the building down on them."

"That's true," Maddox said, nodding. "They don't know we're looking to bring Jora'nal in alive. They might suspect, but if we turn up the heat enough to rattle them, we might just bypass whatever plans they've worked up and make them desperate enough to do something stupid."

"Takal," the AI said across the comm, opening a link to the inventor. "Is it possible to transport us inside the building with the Gulg system?"

"Afraid not," he came back a moment later. "The barrier Geroux reported isn't like a shield. There's no way to punch a hole in it to gain access to the interior of the building. While I could transport you without problem, the issue would be once you arrived. With no way of knowing the layout, I might land you inside a wall or, heaven forbid, a person," he explained. "That would be a horrific way to die, and not instant, I'm afraid."

Reynolds considered it for a second, thinking he could take the chance, but dismissed it immediately.

Even though a glitch in the transport might not kill him, the damage to his android body might be sufficient to cripple him and make it so he was useless even if he survived.

Jiya's plan was their best option.

He nodded at her. "Looks like it's up to you."

"And my little friends," she joked as Geroux handed her three of the programmed mini-drones.

Jiya checked to make sure they were deactivated, then stuffed them inside her armor for safekeeping, hiding them where the armor would best defend them against the barrier's effect.

Once she was ready, she nodded to Reynolds. "Let's do this."

He acknowledged her, then cloaked. Maddox and Ka'nak did the same, and all three of them ran off to approach the building from different angles.

"Be safe," Geroux warned.

"Always." Jiya hugged her friend. "Be back soon."

The first officer cloaked, and Geroux followed suit to keep from being the only one visible once she was left behind.

A creepy silence settled over the street as Jiya waited for the crew to start punching holes in the building.

Reynolds broke the silence first.

He let loose a barrage of weapons fire, blowing holes in the wall to the east, then darted off to find a new location to do it again. Ka'nak and Maddox did the same on opposite sides of the building as Geroux kept watch with the drones to ensure that none of the cultists tried to flee.

Jiya waited as the crew broke through the walls, chewing them apart in random locations to keep the cultists from guessing where they might come through.

Frantic return fire came back at the crew as the cultists tried to stop Reynolds from bringing the building down on them.

Jiya held her ground for a few more seconds, waiting to find the best entry, and when it appeared, she ran as fast as she could and slipped inside. She felt the slight tingle of the barrier being triggered, and she dodged to the side to avoid fire in case the barrier doubled as an alarm system.

She didn't sit still for more than a second as she gained her bearings.

Jiya had emerged in a small room on the west side, which was filled with crates and boxes that looked as if they'd been there a long time. There was the slight whiff of mildew in the air, and Jiya spied mold growing on some of the boxes.

Low-rent bad-guy hideout, check, she remarked in her head as she crept along the floor while Reynolds and Ka'nak continued to blast the building from outside.

At the door to the room, she stopped and listened. Though she could hear little over the explosions of rock and rubble and the furious shouts of the cultists, she didn't believe anyone was stationed just outside the door. She eased it open and peeked, grateful that the door didn't protest its motion.

Beyond it, she saw a large room, mostly barren of furniture, but it became instantly clear she'd made the right choice coming in alone.

There on the floor were dozens of makeshift beds constructed of simple mats with thin sheets, wadded pillows topping each of them off.

Cultists filled the room, weapons at the ready, but only two of them stood near the hole punched in the closest wall, returning fire at Reynolds and the others. From the angle of the hole, it was clear the crew couldn't see inside well enough to realize just how many were crowded into the room.

And it wasn't the only one filled with cultists.

One of them ducked into the room from an adjoining room on the far side of the chamber, leaving the door open in his wake. That room was also covered in bedding, soldiers kneeling all around in tight clusters as they stayed low.

"Draw them in," she heard a cultist she couldn't identify say. "Pull back."

The people did as they were ordered and eased away from the holes in the wall as if retreating, their return fire slowing dramatically. One of the cultists at the far end of the room opened another door, and the disciples backed through it.

Jiya spied even more of the cultists in the far room.

There had to be over fifty she could see, and who knew just how many there were positioned around the rest of the building?

The fire outside came to a halt, and she knew Reynolds and the rest of the crew were pulling back to observe and await her signal.

She thought about going back the way she'd come in and letting them know what she'd found, but that would ruin what little surprise they still had in their favor.

No, she needed to continue with the plan.

Jiya slipped behind a broken set of freestanding shelves and hunkered down. Despite being cloaked, she felt more comfortable there while digging out the drones.

She pulled them out and examined each, activating them with a touch. Two of them sparked to life immediately, but the third had been fried by the barrier. She released the two operational drones to do their work, and they hummed off and disappeared. She stuffed the scorched one back into her armor to make sure it didn't get left behind.

She didn't want the cultists stumbling across it and taking advantage of the tech.

Once it was secured, she crept across the room, angling toward the doorway the last of the cultists had gone through. She inched up to the edge and glanced inside to get the layout of the room.

It was half the size of the room she was in, and there were overturned tables taking up what little space was left after all the cultists had squeezed inside. The disciples, easily twenty of them, crouched behind the tables, using them for cover, and remained quiet as they watched the door she peeked in through. It was the only exit out of the room. Their weapons were trained on the door, and nervous fingers hovered over their triggers. Sweat beaded their brows.

Jiya drew a deep breath at seeing just how many of them there were in the room, not even counting how many were stashed about the rest of the building.

There were simply too many to take them head-on.

Then she had an idea.

CHAPTER FIVE

Jora'nal snarled as his minions reported the arrival of the SD *Reynolds'* crew outside their temporary headquarters.

Explosions rattled the walls moments after. It felt as if they were tearing the building down around him.

Jora'nal growled low in his throat.

While he'd expected them to arrive at some point since Reynolds and his people were wily and resourceful, Jora'nal had believed he'd have more time before they showed up.

He hadn't expected to be cornered, and he hadn't prepared for it.

Now it was too late.

The disciples on Muultar failed him. They had given in to fear and offered Jora'nal's location to the android, and now, here they were.

The *Pillar* had been severely damaged in its last contact with the SD *Reynolds*, and it had taken far longer for him to gather the necessary tools and materials needed to attend to the damage than he had thought it would.

As necessary as it had been to see the *Pillar* fully repaired, Jora'nal regretted that he hadn't packed up and finished the work elsewhere. He'd been too comfortable here.

He'd also trusted the terror evoked by Phraim-'Eh's name to keep the disciples loyal.

That had been his biggest mistake.

And now the enemy was upon them, and he could think of no easy clear way out of this mess.

It didn't help that the SD *Reynolds* had positioned itself in a way that essentially locked the *Pillar* into its berth at the space dock. The only way out would be to fight, if he could even make it back to the ship, and that would trigger the automated response of the Asparian defense system. Being caught in the middle of the dock with all the other ships squeezed in alongside them made that an unenviable proposition.

The *Pillar* could handle the defense system and locals long enough to Gate away before becoming too damaged, but with the SD *Reynolds* looming over them, there was no way that would happen.

At best, his ship would be destroyed after wounding the SD *Reynolds*. At worst, and also the most likely outcome, given that the enemy had armed its most vicious of weapons, the *Pillar* would die a miserable death without dealing a substantive blow in return.

And with Reynolds outside his headquarters, it would only be a matter of time before they made a push inside.

Jora'nal didn't think his minions could take out the android or his people, despite their numerical superiority. He was a rat, trapped in a hole.

He clutched his small computer, which doubled as a communication device, hesitating to activate it. Explosions continued rattling the building as he debated, and Jora'nal knew his time was running out. He had to reach out to the master.

There was no longer a choice in the matter.

Jora'nal triggered the comm program and held his breath as he waited for the device to relay the signal to the hardwired system he'd run beneath the building, triggering the transmission across the Etheric.

Moments seemed to stretch into decades as he waited, but at last, Phraim-'Eh's voice sounded across the Etheric.

"Given you are using the backup communication device, I presume this contact is not of a positive nature," Phraim-'Eh stated, his voice icy.

Jora'nal swallowed hard, clearing his throat before he managed to speak. "Master, the Federation android has found us earlier than predicted," he reported, doing his best to not stutter. "I have enough people to—"

"If you believed you had enough disciples to prevail over them, you would not have dared to reach out to me, now would you?" Phraim-'Eh asked, a snarl evident in his tone.

"No, Master," Jora'nal admitted, hating the terror leaking into his voice.

He bit back a growl at his submissiveness, but he made certain not to let his master hear any of it.

Jora'nal was no coward, but Phraim-'Eh was so much more than he could comprehend. He called himself a god, and Jora'nal believed it.

The things Phraim-'Eh could do frightened him.

He'd once seen his master stroll onto the field of battle and take out a hundred enemies with a single swing of his arm. Death had radiated around him that day, the stench of charred corpses rising in the air as black smoke clawed at his lungs.

Jora'nal would never forget that smell as long as he lived.

And he feared that might not be much longer if he dissatisfied his lord again.

There'd been far too many mistakes already, and the Federation scum finding him so soon was just one more added to the list.

He couldn't see his master forgiving him *this* failure.

"What would you have me do, Master?" Jora'nal asked, knowing he was likely opening the door to his own doom.

Nothing Phraim-'Eh expected would come easy...or painlessly.

His lord was silent for a moment.

Jora'nal swallowed hard, his hand trembling on the small computer, and he worried he might drop it before his lord spoke again.

He wants me afraid, Jora'nal realized to his dismay.

It was working.

It felt as if a hellish eternity had passed before Phraim-'Eh deigned to speak.

His words might well have been an epitaph.

"You will stand your ground, disciple," Phraim-'Eh ordered. "It is in the best interests of your damned soul to adapt and overcome this trial in my name."

The reality of what his master was telling him sank in

hard. Jora'nal's blood went cold in his veins, threatening to bring his heart to a stop.

"You will use whatever means necessary to end the threat of this Federation pawn or, at the very least, you will hold him and his people off until I arrive," his master went on.

Jora'nal stiffened at hearing that.

His god was coming!

"You're coming...here, Master?" Jora'nal's lips quivered as he asked the question. His mind whirled.

"It is clear you are incapable of doing what must be done," Phraim-'Eh explained. "As such, it is up to me if I wish to see success in this matter, and I most certainly intend to succeed. The Federation minion will die, and I will brook no more failures. The Voice will precede me to assess the situation on the ground. Pray that he brings me good news, Jora'nal."

The line disconnected, and Jora'nal was left with his master's threats ringing in his ears.

He would be there soon.

Jora'nal's time was coming to a close.

He stood in place, his thoughts reeling, desperately looking for a way out of his dilemma, but there was little hope he would prevail.

The explosions that had warned of Reynolds' arrival were slowing now, and Jora'nal knew it was only a matter of time before the real attack began. The enemy would spill inside and force Jora'nal on his heels.

That left him little choice.

Jora'nal grunted and cleared his throat, swallowing the fear that had settled over him.

He might not be able to defeat the Federation scum and end their threat, but there was something he *could* do.

He laughed as he imagined it.

Unlike the disciples on Muultar, Jora'nal would not surrender, would not give in and be known as a traitor, giving up his master. No, he would be remembered, if only as a martyr to the cause.

If he couldn't send the android to Hell, he would bring Hell to the android.

CHAPTER SIX

"What's taking her so long?" Reynolds growled, asking no one in particular.

He and the others returned to Geroux's side, everyone staring at the now-smoking building, except for the young tech.

Her gaze was locked on her computer.

The cultists had initially defended the building, but they'd pulled back shortly after. Reynold wasn't entirely sure if it was because they couldn't see an enemy to engage or if Jora'nal was trying to lure them inside, but Reynolds was already tired of waiting.

He had Jora'nal in his grasp, and he wanted to end the puke's life.

"There!" Geroux called a long moment later. "One of the drones has reached the barrier generator. It's flashing its way past the device's security, and I'm getting flutters of scans as the defensive screen fluctuates."

"How much longer until it's down?" Reynolds questioned.

Geroux raised her hand, fingers extended to the sky. She lowered one finger, then another, performing a measured countdown, then she grinned, dropping her hand altogether.

"The barrier is gone," she reported, tapping at her screen to get an updated and complete scan of the building in front of them.

"What are you seeing?" Maddox asked. "Any sign of Jiya?"

"Reports are coming in now and… Oh, hell," Geroux muttered. "Look at this."

Geroux sent the information to the crew.

Dozens upon dozens of red dots, which indicated the dug-in cultists, appeared throughout the building. The place was swarming with them.

The green dot that represented Jiya was stationed in front of a swarm of twenty enemies.

Reynolds reached out to her over the comm.

"You know there's a score of cultists not more than two meters in front of you, right?" the AI asked.

Jiya chuckled. "I do indeed," she replied casually, her voice quiet. "They're in the room next to me, and don't know I'm here. Yet," she added with a low chuckle. "I've been waiting for you to make contact before I did anything stupid."

"Define stupid," Reynolds told her.

"I'm about to make a mess, so get ready to come in," she answered.

Reynolds glanced at the crew. Maddox shrugged, one eyebrow raised.

Ka'nak laughed. "Something's about to go boom!"

Jiya eased two grenades out and inched closer to the door. The cultists remained in place, hunkered down and waiting for the crew to burst in.

The way the building was arranged forced the crew to come into a section of rooms that ran the entire length of the building, which would leave them exposed. The cultists could simply pop out and rain down fire since there would be no one there except for the enemy.

Once the fight started, they could then move out and engage the crew without being so bunched up.

It was an effective tactic.

At least it would have been if Jiya weren't already inside the building.

She triggered the grenades and held them for a moment, then kicked the door open and flung them inside.

Gunfire erupted as soon as she stepped back out, but she'd kicked the door so hard that it hit the wall and bounced back, slamming shut an instant later.

Jiya darted across the room as the grenades went off.

Two loud explosions sounded so close together as to be one, and the door to the room she'd left behind blew open, flames and shrapnel pouring through it as though it were the mouth to hell.

Jiya freed two more grenades as debris clattered behind her.

The far door where she'd seen more of the cultists hide popped open, and a couple of surprised faces looked her way.

She grinned when she remembered they couldn't see her with the cloak activated.

Jiya tossed the grenades into the open room.

The cultists stumbled back as the two weapons materialized out of thin air and tumbled over their heads.

It took them too long to recognize the threat they manifested.

By then, Jiya had pivoted away and around a corner.

The grenades exploded right after.

Whatever screams there might have been were drowned out by the roar.

"I've got their attention," Jiya reported. "Feel free to join me any time."

She shouldered her rifle and peered around the corner, positioning herself to cover the crew as they entered the building.

Cultists stumbled out of the rooms, charred and wounded, and Jiya took them out.

She popped off shot after shot, putting down the injured cultists for good, shifting her aim between the first and second rooms she'd exploded.

Her scanners picked up the rest of the crew entering the building at her back, cloaked, taking advantage of the chaos she had instigated.

Cultists stormed down a flight of stairs at the back of the building, and Reynolds and Maddox turned their fire on them.

Bursts of energy brightened the room, cutting through the smoke of the explosions. The cultists couldn't see the enemy, so they resorted to filling every open space with weapons fire and doing their best to trace the fire coming back their way.

It wasn't the most effective effort, but it was good enough to keep the crew from advancing.

"Stay safe," Reynolds warned as more cultists spilled down a hallway on the opposite side of the room, ramping up the threat level.

"These guys are zealots!" Ka'nak called as the cultists raced forward without fear of dying.

They crowded into the room despite their companions being gunned down all around them.

Bodies hit the floor and were trampled as the other cultists scrambled to get out in the open and be the one to kill the enemy.

Jiya chucked another grenade into the throng as the crew poured it on.

"Fire in the hole!" Jiya warned.

The crew pulled back behind cover as the grenade exploded.

Cultists shrieked and fell to the ground in pieces.

Jiya was grateful for the sound dampeners on her helmet as she squeezed off more rounds at the cluster of cultists.

She had to admire their tenacity if nothing else.

They kept coming, weapons fire ripping up the wall that shielded her.

She ducked back, realizing that her cloak was essentially useless now. With so few places to hide, the cultists had zeroed in on the crew's locations and were massing their fire there.

"Geroux!" Reynolds called. "Watch our six," he told her.

"Scanners are picking up movement outside of the building, circling around and headed our way. Looks to be about fifteen of them."

"On it," the young tech replied, and she darted off, repositioning herself so she could counter anyone trying to engage the crew from behind.

She took a page from Jiya's book and readied a grenade.

The gunfight continued.

Jiya ducked and sprayed around the corner, taking out the legs of several cultists who'd managed to close.

They went down screaming among their brethren, only to have Maddox silence them permanently as Jiya reloaded her weapon.

Scans showed more of the cultists piling up so they could force their way into the room.

Then Jiya heard Geroux's weapon discharge.

There was a muffled explosion outside and debris rattled around, more smoke filling the room.

"That'll dissuade them." Geroux chuckled as she continued to fire, keeping the flanking cultists at bay.

Reynolds darted across the room and repositioned, tossing another grenade down the hall where most of the cultists were coming from.

"I don't see Jora'nal anywhere," he said over the sound of the explosion.

Jiya ducked away for a second, letting the wall take the beating from the blow, then leaned back out to snap shots down the hall.

"There's no clarity to the scans," Maddox stated. "Nothing to indicate which one of these damn red dots is him."

"You think he's sneaking out?" Ka'nak asked.

"He's still here," Geroux reported. "The drones outside have shown no one leaving the building."

"What about those cultists you're holding off?" Ka'nak asked. "Didn't they come from in here?"

"Nope." She shook her head. "They were in one of the surrounding buildings, or nearby. No one's left this place."

"Then we need to clear the building room by room until we find that shifty motherfucker," Reynolds stated. "Let's take the rest of these assholes out and get to finding Jora'nal."

The crew nodded their agreement and turned up the heat on the enemy cultists.

Ka'nak stepped out from behind cover to reposition during a short lull, only to catch a shot to the chest.

The Melowi warrior stumbled backward with a grunt, falling among the debris that cluttered the floor and kicking up dust.

"Ka'nak!" Jiya shouted.

She turned, ready to race over and help him up, but the warrior rolled behind cover and climbed to his feet, dusting himself off.

"I'm good," he called, rejoining the melee. "Armor took the brunt of the shot. Ribs are sore, but I've had worse sparring in the arena." He laughed.

Jiya turned back to the fight and took out two cultists who'd leapt over the piles of dead bodies and charged her in the short time she'd paused to check on Ka'nak.

Both died before they got close.

Maddox darted out from under cover and positioned himself on the ground behind a pile of corpses. With all the smoke, it was nearly impossible for Jiya to see him despite the vague flutter of his cloak on her scanners.

He burrowed into the bodies and inched closer to the other cultists, giving himself a better angle to shoot down the hall.

Jiya covered him, drawing the cultists' fire her way.

Reynolds took advantage of that and eased even closer, throwing another grenade down the hall.

The explosion shook the floor and rained dust down on their heads.

Maddox opened fire in the wake of the grenade, filling the hallway with gunfire and tearing apart what remained of the enemy positioned there. The last of the cultists out in the open were gunned down.

"Help Geroux clear our way out, Ka'nak," Reynolds ordered.

The warrior spun away, stationed himself at another of the holes in the wall, and began raining fire through it.

"Jiya! You and Maddox on me," the AI called, waving them on.

Both complied and followed Reynolds down the wrecked hallway, each doing their best to avoid stomping on the remnants of dead bodies.

However, there were simply too many of them.

Jiya felt the cultists beneath her feet as she and the crew advanced down the hall. It wasn't exactly a pleasant experience, she had to admit, but this was war.

It's what happened.

Besides, the cultists had earned their deaths.

They'd done nothing but sow terror and pain across the

universe, and Jiya didn't feel the slightest bit of remorse for what she had to do.

Once they'd traversed the hall, the crew realized there was a door off to the side of the stairwell that had provided access to the room for the cultists.

The crew positioned themselves so they could cover both, and Jiya scanned the upper floors. She picked up another fifteen cultists making their way toward the crew.

"I've got a group coming down on our heads," she reported. "They're positioning to target this area. If we advance, we'll be in their line of fire."

"And there are another twenty or so in the rooms behind this door," Reynolds told them.

"We could toss more grenades," Maddox suggested.

Reynolds shook his head. "We risk taking out Jora'nal that way."

Maddox shrugged, showing how little he cared about the enemy alien, but the general understood they needed the bastard alive.

The door was flung open then, and a cold voice emerged from inside.

"Unless you all want to die, I suggest you deactivate your cloaking devices and back off."

Jiya recognized the voice as Jora'nal's.

An overweight cultist eased out into the hall, and Jiya stared at the male. It took her a second to realize that he wasn't actually fat, he had something wrapped about his torso.

Explosives!

A second and third cultist crept out, and Reynolds signaled for the crew to uncloak.

There wasn't much point in being invisible then since there was nowhere for the crew to slip past without colliding with a cultist and triggering the explosives.

At a signal from the AI, the crew backed up, moving toward the front room they'd entered the building through.

"Heads up," Reynolds warned Geroux and Ka'nak as they moved back toward them. "We've got cultists with enough explosives to bring this entire building down. Stay cloaked, but *do not* engage."

"Fucking great," Ka'nak grunted.

The group of cultists upstairs started down, and they, too, were swathed in explosives. They grinned wildly as they displayed the bombs they'd proudly strapped to their bodies.

More spilled from the door down below, all primed like the others, then Jora'nal stepped out behind them, using the throng of booby-trapped cultists as a shield.

"Did you think it would be so easy to kill me, Reynolds?" Jora'nal asked.

The AI shrugged. "I'd hoped."

Jora'nal chuckled, continuing to advance behind his disciples.

"I must give you credit," Jora'nal went on. "I had expected the disciples of Muultar to show their lord more loyalty and remain quiet. Your torture tactics must be quite refined to have broken them so quickly."

Reynolds shook his head. "We don't torture anyone, no matter how much they deserve it."

Jora'nal raised an eyebrow, clearly not believing the AI. "Then how—"

"Amazing what landing a superdreadnought on top of their homes will do for morale." Maddox laughed.

Jora'nal snorted, clearly disappointed in his people.

"How...unfortunate," he muttered. "I had hoped our disciples would prove more capable than that."

"Hope in one hand, shit in the other," Ka'nak told him. "See which one fills up faster."

Jora'nal snarled at the Melowi.

"No matter, though," the cultist went on as he eased forward, he and his weaponized disciples filling the room in front of the crew. "We were prepared for you."

Reynolds laughed. "Which is why you trapped yourself in a building with no alternate exits and your people are strapped with explosives," the AI said. "Sounds more like we caught you with your pants down around your ankles, and you're trying to make yourself feel better about recreating the Alamo."

Jora'nal growled. "I have no idea what this 'Alamo' you refer to is, but it is you who are staring down your defeat, you who are trapped in this place."

He lifted a small computer so the crew could see it clearly. His finger sat heavily on a button.

"We've gathered enough explosives to turn a ten-block radius into a smoking crater. I've only to release this button, and all of us become dust," he warned.

"Except you want something," Reynolds told him, "or you would have already detonated your bombs and ended this farce."

"You know nothing of what I want!" Jora'nal shrieked, shoving the device in their direction as if threatening to blow them all up.

Jiya heard the quaver in his voice, the uncertainty, and saw the shaking of his hand. They might not know what he was after, but she sure as shit knew he didn't want to die.

"Well, here's your chance to tell us," Reynolds went on, ignoring the cultist's histrionics. "What do you want, Jora'-nal? Enlighten us."

"You will let me pass and return to my ship," he advised, then pointed at Jiya. "I will take her with us to ensure your compliance."

"Not going to happen, fuckwad," Reynolds snarled. "You don't get to demand terms, and you sure as shit don't get to walk off with one of my crew."

"Then you put all of your crew at risk," Jora'nal stated. "I have advised the *Pillar* to engage your ship, Reynolds, and I have numerous allies among the locals who will gladly join the fight."

Reynolds stared at the cultist, wondering if he was bluffing.

A message from the SD *Reynolds* made it clear that he wasn't.

"The *Pillar* is turning on us," Asya reported. "It looks ready to fire, Captain."

"The ESD still charging?" Reynolds questioned.

"We've been holding it stable, but it's been on too long, and it's drawing too much power. If we let loose with it now, we'll be vulnerable to attack from the station and the other ships out here since half our systems will short out," Asya told him.

"Adjust it down," Reynolds ordered, "but keep it available. We're going to need the SD *Reynolds* functional."

"Yes, sir," she answered.

"Stand by," the AI told her, then turned his glare back on Jora'nal as the alien went on.

"Your time is running out, android," Jora'nal warned. His finger trembled on the button. He looked ready to release his hold any second now. "I walk away, or we all die, here and now."

It was clear to Jiya that he didn't expect to make it out of this alive.

She stared back and forth between the two opponents. Reynolds didn't want to back down, and she suspected Jora'nal simply wouldn't. His only way out of here was if the AI let him go.

If it weren't for the crew standing there, she figured Reynolds would force Jora'nal's hand, but he would have to be more careful with them hovering about.

So, rather than let Reynolds do something he'd regret just so he could keep them safe, Jiya decided to act.

"Asya! Transport all of us to the ship!" she called over the comm. "Now!"

Knowing she only had a split-second before Asya complied, Jiya darted right as obviously as she could, cloaked, then changed direction, leaping to her left.

Straight at Jora'nal.

The alien stiffened, not having expected the sudden rush. He panicked, realizing he couldn't see where she'd gone.

By then, it was too late.

She collided with the alien as his finger came loose from the device.

Jiya slammed an armored elbow into Jora'nal's face, smashing his nose and knocking him unconscious. He slumped in her arm as she grabbed the small computer before it could tumble away.

A loud roar rattled her skull, and she felt the heat of the explosives detonating.

Then she felt nothing.

CHAPTER SEVEN

The crew appeared on the bridge of the SD *Reynolds*, clattering to the deck in a heap.

Reynolds scrambled to his feet and raced over to Jiya. She grinned at him, clutching both of her trophies: the computer, and a limp Jora'nal.

"Secure him," Reynolds ordered, pointing at the cultist.

"Gladly," Maddox replied with a grin.

The general and Ka'nak jumped to the task, clutching the cultist and dragging him off the bridge before he had a chance to regain consciousness.

Geroux helped her friend to her feet and snatched up Jora'nal's small computer. She made sure her friend was okay before retiring to her station to examine the device.

The SD *Reynolds* shuddered as the *Pillar* opened fire, its attack sparking across the gravitic shields.

"Take that motherfucker out!" Reynolds commanded, pointing at the enemy ship.

Tactical was all too willing to comply.

Railguns rattled and peppered the *Pillar*'s shields as

Tactical let loose with everything he had except for the ESD.

"Guess there's not much need for the tracking rounds anymore," Asya said.

Reynolds shrugged. "Things didn't exactly go as planned, but better to be prepared than not," he replied.

"The *Pillar* is still a tough son of a bitch," XO said as the enemy ship was bombarded. "We still might need those tracking rounds if it survives this."

"Make sure it doesn't," Reynolds advised. "We've got Jora'nal. He'll lead us to his master."

"The defense system is firing on both of us!" Ria reported as the SD *Reynolds* rattled, its shields deflecting the majority of the incoming fire.

"Enemy ships gearing up and turning our way," XO called.

"Guess he did have some friends here after all," Reynolds remarked.

"More likely just opportunists looking to score points or get a chance to scavenge the wreck of a superdreadnought," Asya said. "Either way, we can't have them pecking at us."

The ship shuddered again.

"I agree," Reynolds told her.

"The *Pillar* has its starboard flank to us," Tactical announced. "If ever there was a time to use the ESD, now would be it."

Reynolds nodded without hesitation. "Minimize all systems to keep us from blowing a fuse," he ordered. "Ensign Alcott, get us out of range of that damn planetary defense system. That's the biggest threat right now outside of the *Pillar*."

"Yes, sir!" Ria replied, immediately maneuvering the SD *Reynolds* back, opening up space between the defense rig and the ship and pulling them out of orbit.

"Do it, Tactical," Reynolds shouted.

The lights on the bridge dimmed, half of the viewscreens going dark as the SD *Reynolds* lowered its ship-wide energy usage to minimize the impact of firing the ESD.

Everything around him seemed to hum as the weapon was ramped up to full again, the system recovering from the long process of idling as they covered the *Pillar* while the crew was dirtside.

That the weapon had been prepared was both a good and bad thing, and Reynolds wasn't completely sure how it would affect the weapon's performance, having had it on for so long.

As it turned out, he didn't need to worry.

The weapon reached critical mass and sent deadly beams of energy racing through the SD *Reynolds'* systems. Insulated against the energy as well as possible, Reynolds still felt the drain on the ship, but what he felt more was satisfaction.

As the energy surged and spilled from the SD *Reynolds*, he felt the ESD's power running true and pure.

The beam erupted and ripped through the shields of the *Pillar* as though they weren't there. There was a brilliant flash as the shields gave way and the blast slammed into the vulnerable hull of the enemy superdreadnought.

"*Fuck*, yeah!" Tactical shouted as he angled the ESD to do as much damage as possible.

The beam trailed along the hull of the *Pillar*, wreaking havoc everywhere it touched and beyond.

Several sections of the Asparian defense rig were shredded by the weapon, great slabs of steel melting and peeling away from the whole.

The *Pillar* listed, appearing to split in half horizontally. Brilliant flares went off along its length, and then it exploded.

Debris erupted in all directions, shredding the dock and many of the ships berthed there, creating a chain reaction of destruction.

Since the SD *Reynolds* was too strained to Gate, Reynolds called for Ensign Alcott to put as much distance between them and the planet as possible.

"On it!" she replied.

Debris and enemy weapons fire pelted the gravitic shields, each blow causing the ship's lights to flicker.

"Turn the weapons on those pirate ships," Reynolds ordered.

"Already done," Tactical shouted back as the SD *Reynolds'* energy slowly climbed toward normal.

The viewscreens showed three of the local ships headed their way, shields up and firing.

It was a bold move given what they'd just witnessed, Reynolds felt.

"Angling shields forward to deflect their attacks," Ria called. "All primary systems are online, and secondary are recycling, coming back up. We've got about sixty seconds before all systems are operational."

Tactical blew one of the alien ships away and turned the railguns on another. Flashes of light peppered their shields as the enemy ship careened toward them.

A few seconds later, the second ship lost its shields. The entire forward section wasn't far behind as Tactical lit it up, tearing it open as if it were a tin can. Atmosphere vented in a rush, and the ship tumbled end over end into the bleakness of space.

The SD *Reynolds'* guns were turned on the last of the ships brave enough to come after them, and that seemed to be enough of a deterrent for it to call off its attack.

Its shields flared as it retreated, Tactical not letting them off the hook that easily. He fired on it until it reached the cover of the Asparian dock.

Ria turned the SD *Reynolds* about and shot off into space as the ship recovered from the use of the ESD.

Once they were clear and it was determined that no other ships from the planet were approaching to challenge them, Reynolds turned to the crew.

He was proud of them.

"Excellent work, people," he said, smiling. "Part of our objective is complete. We blew the fuck out of that piece of shit superdreadnought—"

"And by *we*, he means *me*," Tactical clarified with a chuckle.

"And we captured Jora'nal," the AI went on, ignoring Tactical. "Now, all we need to do is get that weaselly scumbag to tell us where Phraim-'Eh is, and we've completed our mission."

"You think he'll talk to us?" XO wondered.

"Maybe," Reynolds replied, although he had his doubts.

"The guy wants to live, that much is clear. If we can assure him that we're going to take out his master, and Jora'nal won't have to answer for being a disloyal piece of shit, I think there's a good chance we can get him to spill his master's location."

"We might not need him to," Geroux said, interrupting.

The AI spun to her, eyes narrow as he considered what she meant.

She held up the small computer Jiya had taken from Jora'nal.

"This is a multipurpose device," she started to explain. "It's got a ton of stuff in its memory, and it looks well-used. I'm betting everything we need is hidden inside."

"Can you access it?" Jiya asked.

"It's encrypted," Geroux admitted, "but it's hardly on the level of the Gulg coding. I'll be able to break it," she assured them.

"How long?" Reynolds asked.

Geroux shrugged. "Already working on breaking the encryption, but you never know with this kind of thing. There are no self-destructs on it, so unless the defenses become more difficult as I go along, I should have this whole drive mapped out in a day or two at most."

Reynolds nodded. "Okay, you focus on that. Take it to the lab and get Takal to help, if you need it. I want to know everything that computer holds."

"Yes, sir," Geroux replied, hopping up and leaving the bridge, whistling. The doors hissed shut behind her.

"Jiya, come with me," Reynolds told her. "We're going to go have a talk with Jora'nal now that we have him locked up. Can't hurt to work both angles, the computer and the asshole."

"That sounds a bit perverse." Jiya chuckled.

"What do you want the rest of us to do?" XO asked.

"Ensign Alcott, set a course for Grindlevik 3," he answered. "Comm, let Gorad know we're stopping in for a visit and not to shoot us."

"We're going to see that old AI?" Tactical muttered.

"It's as good a place as any to bide our time while we ready our next move," Reynolds replied. "Besides, we can look in and see how things have progressed since we were there last."

"I guess." Reynolds could almost hear Tactical shrug.

"You think Phraim-'Eh is going to come looking for Jora'nal?" XO wondered.

"Doesn't seem like the type of thing a god would do," Reynolds replied, shrugging, "but who the fuck knows with this guy? He hasn't exactly shown himself to be sane so far."

"I'll drop a cloaked probe to monitor the activity in the system and to scan for Kurtherian energy signatures," XO said. "Doubt we'll be able to assess much if one or two ships show up, but I'm thinking Phraim-'Eh's going to bring an army with him if he nuts up enough to come at us in person."

"Do that," Reynolds told him. "And use the Gulg system to keep us linked to it, so we're not showing our hand and giving off Federation energy signals showing that we're monitoring the system."

"Roger that," XO replied.

Reynolds turned to Jiya and ushered her toward the doors, which opened at his gesture.

"Let's go chat up our new friend."

The pair left the bridge and made their way to the brig, which was where Maddox and Ka'nak had taken Jora'nal. They were waiting outside his cell.

The alien sulked in the corner, crusted blood covering his nose and mouth and coloring his chin red.

"We had Dr. Reynolds check him out," Maddox reported as they arrived. "Other than a shattered nose and a busted ego, he's uninjured. Doc wouldn't even bother to clean him up."

Reynolds laughed at his other personality. He would have done the same.

Jora'nal looked up at the sound of Reynolds' amusement. He sneered, which started his nose bleeding again. He let it drip on his chest without so much as a glance.

"So, you have me," he said with a shrug. "It's hardly a victory, especially since you claim you are unwilling to torture a combatant. Surely you don't expect me to hand over the location of my master simply because you ask nicely, do you?" He chuckled, bits of crusty blood falling to the ground before him.

"You're right, I don't intend to torture you," Reynolds agreed.

He dismissed Maddox and Ka'nak with a wave. The two left the brig, heading back to the bridge.

"The truth is, if you know anything, you'll gladly tell us without us ever having to harm so much as an ass-hair on you," Reynolds continued after he and Jiya were alone with the alien.

Jora'nal's eyes narrowed as he stared at the AI. "Unlike

those fools on Muultar, I will not turn on my master. I am a loyal servant to my lord, Phraim—"

"Blah, blah, Phraim-'Eh, fucking blah," Reynolds said, interrupting his pledge of fealty to his would-be god. "Phraim-'Eh isn't here, and I can't imagine he would be all that happy with you if he were. I'm fairly certain this failure to take us out has burned the last bridge between you and your master. Am I right?"

Jora'nal stiffened in his seat, but he was unwilling to admit to anything.

Reynolds hadn't really expected him to, though.

"Not only did you fail to kill us, but you also got your ship, the *Pillar*, destroyed," Jiya said with a grin. "That leaves you zero for two, not even counting letting us off the hook the first time we tangled. Your boss is going to be seriously pissed with you."

"He understands—"

"That you're an idiot?" Reynolds asked.

"A moron?" Jiya added.

"A total fucking abject failure?" Reynolds went on.

"Utterly worthless?" Jiya said with a smile. "Pathetic?" she added.

Jora'nal leapt to his feet, growling. "I am Jora'nal, disciple of Phraim-'Eh, and I will not—"

"You won't survive this," Reynolds told him bluntly, cutting him off. "You know you won't."

"We kill you, or your master does," Jiya explained. "Either way, your part in all of this is done. *You're* done."

They let that sink in for a moment.

Jora'nal stood his ground, glaring at the pair for several

quiet minutes, then he slumped onto the hard, metal bench, the only luxury provided him in the cell.

"Unless..." Reynolds teased.

"Unless I turn on my master and tell you where he is?" Jora'nal scoffed. "Do you think I would do that?"

"I think you're a survivor," Reynolds countered. "I think you'd do almost anything to survive, or you wouldn't be in the position you're in now."

"You don't know anything about me," Jora'nal argued.

Reynolds shrugged. "Maybe not, but I've met a ton of assholes like you," he explained. "You brag and you bluster and threaten, but at the end of the day, all you want to do is get out in one piece."

"We can make that happen," Jiya pressed.

"And all I need to do is betray my god and all my convictions," he replied, shaking his head.

"Convictions don't mean shit when you're dead," Jiya shot back.

"Besides, it's not as if you're our only option," Reynolds told him.

Jora'nal straightened in his seat, pressing his back against the wall, eyes wide. "What do you mean?"

"When Jiya here plowed into you back on Aspar, she grabbed your computer as well as you," Reynold explained.

"No! That's not—"

"Believe it or not, but you weren't conscious enough to know for a fact one way or the other," Jiya goaded. "We're working on decrypting it as we speak, and I have a pretty good idea that we'll find everything we need on there."

"That means we won't need you, in case that wasn't clear," Reynolds went on.

Jora'nal swallowed loud enough for them to hear him. He clambered to his feet.

"There is nothing on that device that will help you," he said.

It was obvious he was lying.

Reynolds shrugged. "If nothing else, the hardline call you made will give us a damn good starting location, seeing as how you can't encrypt information like that while using such old low-tech systems."

Jora'nal stiffened. Beads of sweat appeared on his brow.

"You have until this time tomorrow, or until we finish breaking the encryption on your device, before we decide what to do with you," Reynolds warned. "Be smart, and I'll find some compassion deep inside my metallic heart. We'll dump you off at the ass-end of the universe and you can start your pitiful life over. Stay loyal to your *god*, and you better hope there's some sort of Heaven awaiting you after all this."

Reynolds spun on his heel and marched out of the brig. Jiya looked at the cultist, offering him one last chance to cave before she left.

When he didn't start talking, she shrugged and waved. "See you soon."

She left the brig, the door hissing shut behind her.

She and Reynolds headed back toward the bridge.

"You think he'll crack?" Jiya asked as they walked.

"Probably not," Reynolds admitted. "He's as much a zealot as any of Phraim-'Eh's cult. He probably thinks there's redemption for him if he stays loyal and his master kills us."

"He can't be that stupid, can he?" Jiya asked.

"It's more that he's been brainwashed to believe this Phraim-'Eh is really a god," Reynolds told her. "Despite all our successes against them, Jora'nal can't yet picture that we can win out against his master."

"Then why not give up the guy's location if we're just going to die there?" Jiya wondered.

"Catch-22," Reynolds answered. "If he tells us where Phraim-'Eh is, he betrays his master, regardless of the outcome. His only hope is that Phraim-'Eh takes us out and Jora'nal manages to survive the encounter, which he expects to happen on his master's terms."

Jiya grunted. "That is kind of a slim hope to be dangling from."

"It's the kind of thing zealots believe in," the AI told her. "He's expecting a miracle."

"He better be ready for disappointment." Jiya chuckled.

Reynolds nodded.

"Go get some rest," he told her. "We'll be in the Grindlevik System soon, and we really can't do much until Jora'nal caves or Geroux hacks his computer. Either way, this is likely to be the only downtime we have anytime soon."

Jiya nodded and started toward her quarters. "Beep me if anything interesting happens."

Reynolds waved to her and kept walking.

Today had been a great success, capturing Jora'nal and destroying the *Pillar*, but there was still more to come, and he needed to be ready.

For now, though, he had an AI to visit.

CHAPTER EIGHT

The SD *Reynolds* slipped into Grindlevik space, and Ria gasped at how different the planet looked.

"Wow!" she muttered. "That's amazing."

Where the old defensive perimeter had been, there was now a shiny new one. It looked ominous.

Unlike before, when the defense ring was flanked by destroyers, the ring pulsed with energy, projecting what appeared to be a force field over the entirety of the planet.

The ring had numerous weapons installations apparent across its breadth, and the SD *Reynolds*' scanners picked up its threat as soon as they popped into the system.

"The old boy's gone and upgraded," Tactical said.

"Looks that way," Reynolds replied, examining the energy signatures and grinning as he noted they no longer put off the same kind of Kurtherian identifiers as the last rig had.

Just beyond the barrier loomed what Reynolds knew could only be a Gate under construction.

It was far from finished, not even the frame entirely

constructed yet, but Reynolds could see automated bots and ships circling it, a slow but relentless push of effort being put into the creation.

It would be years before it was finished, but Reynolds was impressed by how far the AI had come already.

"Gorad's evolving," Reynolds commented.

"Speaking of Gorad, he's hailing us," XO announced.

"Onscreen," Reynolds replied.

A second later, the viewscreen flickered and a familiar android face appeared.

"Back so soon, Reynolds?" Gorad asked. "You run out of universe to explore already?"

"And here you thought he wouldn't be happy to see us," Tactical joked. "You were clearly wrong."

"Figured we'd drop in and hang out for a bit, "Reynolds replied. "I recall us making an agreement regarding our stopping by and being provided safe haven and supplies." He raised an eyebrow, jokingly questioning Gorad's commitment.

"To be fair, I'd hoped it was only lip service I was providing," Gorad replied, showing metallic teeth as he grinned.

Reynolds chuckled. "Sorry to ruin your day."

Gorad waved the sarcasm off. "You are, of course, always welcome here. Follow the prompts my people send you, and we'll bring you down to the planet in style."

"Your people?" Jiya asked, surprised.

Gorad smiled. "Much has changed here," he answered. "You'll see it all soon enough."

Reynolds motioned for Ria to take them in once they received the coordinates.

"See you soon," he told Gorad.

The other AI nodded and cut the link.

Seconds later, a Grindlovian voice came over the speakers, providing the coordinates.

Jiya smiled at hearing an authentic voice rather than Gorad's android one.

"Guess he was right about the place changing," she exclaimed.

"Well, he didn't say things had been made better," Tactical demurred. "Otherwise we'd be following the directions of an automated system. Looks like all he's done is plug meatbags into place."

"I'll plug *you* into place," Jiya warned, laughing.

Reynolds turned his attention to the energy sphere that protected the planet, and he grinned as a small section, just large enough to accommodate the SD *Reynolds*, opened. The ship approached it under Ria's control.

"We're being scanned," XO reported, "but not deeply."

Reynolds chuckled. "We've been through this before. Gorad knows what we're packing, but this is likely a first for the physical crew he has manning the defense ring entry."

The AI pointed to a section outside the ship and zoomed the screen in. Geroux clapped when she spotted the mixed faces of Grindlovians and Telluride staring at them out of a massive window on the ring.

"They're standing up!" Jiya noted. "That's amazing!"

The last time the SD *Reynolds* had been there, the Grindlovians had been crippled by their extreme apathy when it came to day to day mundanity. They had spent their lives bound to electric chairs, the Telluride serving their every wish and whim.

That clearly wasn't the case anymore.

There was an equal split of races in the control room they passed, and Jiya was happy to see the two groups getting along and working side by side.

"Shuttle incoming," Ria reported once they were through the shield and it had closed behind them. "Detecting lifeforms aboard."

"He sure is taking this integration idea to the max, huh?" Tactical grunted. "'A meatbag for every occasion' should be his new slogan."

"Or 'One less AI to micromanage everything,'" Jiya snapped back, laughing.

"You wound me," Tactical muttered.

"I wish," she told him as the shuttle entered the hangar bay and settled in, waiting for them.

"You've got the conn, XO," Reynolds told him. "We're all heading down for a look-see."

"Have fun storming the planet," Tactical replied.

Reynolds, Asya, Jiya, and Ria left the bridge and made their way to the hangar bay. San Roche and L'Eliana joined General Maddox, Takal, Geroux, Ka'nak, who were already there.

"This is one hell of an adventure," Ka'nak said, looking at the entire crew. "I can't remember the last time all of us went dirtside together. Shit, even Ria is going."

The ensign shrugged. "I like my job. What can I say?"

Jiya grabbed the girl and tugged her over beside her and Geroux. "Don't let that brute tell you how to live your life. Do what makes you happy."

"Yet I'm regularly told not to drink," Takal said with a sly grin.

"Just get in the shuttle," Geroux playfully barked, pushing Takal up the ramp.

"I'm going, I'm going," the inventor said, raising his arms in surrender.

A few minutes later, the entire crew was seated and strapped in, and the shuttle lifted off, exiting the hangar bay, and returning to Grindlevik 3.

Jiya stared at the pilots as the shuttle descended.

It was two Grindlovians, a male and a female.

One caught her staring and smiled at her.

"This is fantastic," Jiya told the female. "I love seeing you pilot the craft. What's your name?"

"I'm Fulla Hirvin, and my co-pilot is Vor Gerfur," she answered. "There are many of us now." She gestured to her legs, which appeared almost normal, although there was still the slightest bit of atrophy remaining. They looked thin. "My people work many of the jobs that require a technical mind and a slightly less athletic body. We have become pilots and executives, and all manner of workers."

Geroux clapped, grinning.

Jiya noticed they wore plain uniforms, but there were hints of Telluride in the design, bright patches at the shoulders and collars. It was subtle—Jiya presumed that was because it was a work uniform—but the influence of the other race on the planet was definitely there.

"It's good to see that things are working out," Jiya told her.

"We'll be on the ground soon. Then you can see the

full extent of what your visit opened up for us." She turned back to the console, and Jiya let her work in silence.

Not long after, the ship was on the ground and the hatch was open, ramp down.

The crew stepped out onto the tarmac of what might as well have been another world than the one they'd last visited.

Where there had been nothing but automated vehicles darting back and forth across the landing field, doing all the menial labor and repairs, there was now a virtual explosion of Grindlovians and Telluride.

They worked in unison, loading and unloading supplies and equipment, clambering over the ships parked there, making repairs or adjustments, and much more Jiya didn't recognize.

Some of the Grindlovians were using the powered leg devices she'd seen them in last, aiding their speed and movement, but it was clear these were being used as an enhancement, not a requirement.

The Grindlovians looked healthy and strong, and though they couldn't compete with the Telluride at this stage of their evolution, it was clear they were determined to try.

As the crew stared, taking the new world in, a vehicle approached and parked alongside them. Gorad sat in the driver's seat. His android body had been upgraded since they'd seen him last, although the basic features remained the same, providing a nice constant.

The other AI waved them in.

"Good to see you, Reynolds," Gorad said. "And you too,

San Roche and L'Eliana," he told his people, who'd gone into space with Reynolds.

The pair grinned and waved, clearly happy to be home, if only for a short while.

"It's good to see you, too, Gorad," the other AI replied, smirking.

The crew clambered into the vehicle, and it started off.

Jiya noted that even the AI seemed to be doing things manually more than before. There were actual controls in front of him that he manipulated.

The ride into Goranton was quick but telling all the same.

No longer was the Grindlevik 3 society split into two parts. The crew marveled at seeing a mix of races walking along the sidewalks, Telluride and Grindlovians inter-acting as equals rather than masters and servants.

There were some of the powered chairs here and there, but not many. A couple were even being used by Telluride, the squat, powerful people having altered the vehicles to fit their bigger frames comfortably.

Those in the chairs, however, didn't look weak. They simply looked to be taking advantage of the opportunity to sit and relax while traveling about their day-to-day business.

The surrounding buildings showed the same evolution. Where everything had been a horrid gray outside the Telluride part of town, now color was everywhere. There were still smatterings of gray here and there, but there had been an obvious merging of the two styles.

Art decorated many of the surfaces, and it was clear to Jiya that it wasn't only being produced by the Telluride, based on the style. Grindlovians had clearly been hard at work decorating their homes and businesses.

Ria stared at everything, wide-eyed and curious.

"Strange sight, is it not?" Gorad asked as they pulled into the compound that housed the AI.

"It is, indeed," Reynolds admitted. "I'm amazed by how quickly the two sides have reconciled and come together."

Gorad parked the vehicle and climbed out, ushering the crew after him. He made his way to his compound, and although the doors opened of their own accord, a nicely dressed Grindlovian greeted them and waved the group inside.

Much like everywhere else, the plain outpost had been altered, color and lights all over the place and art decorating the walls, making the compound far more welcoming that it had been before.

"Things are not yet perfect," Gorad admitted as he led the crew into what had been the council chambers the last time they'd been there, "but we are certainly on our way to a pleasant parity I could never have imagined before your arrival."

Reynolds smiled, glad he and the crew could help them better their world.

That had been the plan all along.

As they entered the room, Jiya noticed that the council chambers had also been renovated.

She didn't see any of the portals in the floor that allowed for the Grindlovian council to rise up out of it. Now, long seats like pews lined the room, leading to a casual set of tables at the front. She recognized some of the people sitting there.

L'Willow was there, and L'Sofee stood behind her in a position of support.

She hadn't wanted to be part of the council, but had chosen to help lead her people through the changes to come. Jiya smiled, realizing the Telluride female still remained strong in her convictions.

However, none of the original Grindlovians sat on the council any longer. Jiya was surprised to see new faces she didn't know.

"Come in and have a seat," Gorad told them.

The group ran over and dished out friendly hugs and greetings to the Telluride they knew, San Roche and L'Eliana garnering the most excited of them. They were then introduced to the Grindlovians on the council.

"This is Vor Tye, Fulla Ni, and Fulla Bel." L'Sofee gestured to each in turn.

"Pleasure to meet you all," Jiya said, speaking for the entire crew.

And she meant it.

There was none of the lingering hostility that had been there before, the Grindlovians holding tight to their positions and power.

Those in their spots now were happy, and had obviously benefited from the change in society. They looked fit, and had none of the sunken cheeks or apathetic slump about them that had previously defined the Grindlovians.

The shift was startling.

The crew mingled and chatted away as Reynolds and Gorad spoke.

"Have you rid yourself of the cult yet?" Gorad asked.

Reynolds shook his head. "Not yet, but we're working

on it. We just captured the bastard who's been following us around in a superdreadnought and destroyed his ship. Now we're working on finding his master and ending it for good. That's part of the reason we've stopped by."

Gorad nodded. "What can I help you with?"

Reynolds waved Geroux over. She plodded up a moment later.

"Show Gorad the computer we got from Jora'nal," Reynolds told her.

She produced it, handing it over to the android.

"It has complex security encryption," Reynolds explained. "It's one we'll break quickly enough, but I figured we could kill three birds with one stone and rest here on Grindlevik 3 while we avoid being a target of the cult, as well as getting your help speeding up the encryption-breaking," the AI said. "With all of us working on it, I think we can hack it within a few hours."

Gorad remained silent as he examined the small computer, turning it on and watching the scroll of information across the screen. He made a face as he looked, identifying the code and security aspects.

"I think this will be easy enough with all of us chipping away at it," he agreed. "This isn't anywhere near as complex as other codes I've seen, but it has an interesting feature: a resurrecting code wall."

Geroux nodded. "That's what's slowing me down. Every time I hack one of the firewalls, another one pops up at the end of the line, forcing me to adjust and come at it a different way. I just can't seem to get past more than one or two at a time before another is put into place."

"This is definitely a system that requires speed to crack

it and shut off the resurrection code before it can respawn firewalls," Gorad noted. "With all three of us tied into the system, chipping away at different firewalls so they drop all at the same time, it shouldn't be a problem."

"Then let's get to work...if you don't mind," Reynolds said.

Gorad shook his head. "Not at all. We should have this cracked before dinner."

"Did someone say dinner?" Ka'nak asked from across the room.

"I did indeed." Gorad laughed as he ushered everyone out of the room. "Please, dear council, take our guests to see what changes their presence has wrought on our world, and we three will work the puzzle of this device." He held up the computer.

Reynolds nodded to the crew when they looked his way for approval. "Oh, and, Takal, do not wander too far. I want you and Gorad to sit down and go over your project with Xyxl and provide his thoughts."

"I'll be available when he is," Takal assured the AI. "Both Xyxl and I would appreciate his input."

Reynolds nodded and waved the crew on to enjoy themselves. There was work to be done, but it would be good for the crew to relax as much as possible.

Given what was coming, he had no idea when the next battle would start or when it would end.

Whenever it happened, he wanted to be ready.

And they *would* be.

CHAPTER NINE

"The Voice is hailing you, Master," one of Phraim-'Eh's disciples told him, easing open the door to his chambers after being invited in.

Phraim-'Eh growled, knowing, much as he had with Jora'nal, that an unexpected message was never good news.

"Route the call through on my private channel," he told the disciple, who muttered his assurances that he would before darting from the room, closing the door behind him with reverent silence.

It was but a few seconds later when the monitor buzzed. Phraim-'Eh waited a moment before activating the comm.

"I am not in the mood to be disappointed, Voice," Phraim-'Eh told his servant, the edges of the words sharp.

"My sincerest apologies, Master, but I have grave news," the Voice answered, and Phraim-'Eh could hear the terror in his warbling tone.

"I expected no less," Phraim-'Eh stated, biting back his frustration at the utter incompetence of his disciples.

How difficult can it be to destroy a Federation superdread-nought and its crew?

"I have received a report that Jora'nal is dead," the Voice went on.

Phraim-'Eh grunted and closed his eyes, reining in his fury. It would do him no good to unleash his rage while aboard his command vessel, the *Godhand*.

When Phraim-'Eh said nothing, the Voice went on.

"Disciples remaining behind tell me that the crew of the SD *Reynolds* attacked him in his headquarters on the planet, trapping him inside."

"I know all this, Voice," the god told his disciple. "Tell me something I do not."

"The Federation crew blew the place up without mercy, taking out nearly all of our people on Aspar as well as a portion of the city in their eagerness to lay waste to Jora'-nal. What foothold we had there is now gone, only a handful of your worshipers remaining alive." The Voice swallowed hard. "And—"

"There is more?" Phraim-'Eh asked, and he could hear the Voice struggling to speak despite the distance.

"The *Pillar* has also been destroyed, Master," the Voice informed him. "The SD *Reynolds* struck it down before slipping away in the aftermath of their destructive visit."

"Were they followed? Do we know where they have gone?"

"No, I'm afraid not, Master. We had no one there tasked to do so, and no other ships in the area, so we have no idea where they Gated to. It could be anywhere, and without the *Pillar*, we have no way of tracking them."

"You seem to have ignored my disinterest in disappointment today," Phraim-'Eh said, growling low in his throat.

The *Godhand* trembled beneath him as his power fought to be free. He pulled the reins of his will tighter and resisted the urge to tear his ship down around him.

He said nothing for a long while, and the Voice knew better than to break the lingering silence.

Only when Phraim-'Eh felt he could control his temper did he speak again.

"How near are you to Aspar?"

"I can be there within a few hours," the Voice answered. Phraim-'Eh heard the question in his voice before he even spoke it. "But with Jora'nal gone, do you still need me there?"

"I do," the god answered. "Jora'nal was a fool. He left us no means to track the Federation superdreadnought, and I have no faith in his effort to obfuscate his tracks, let alone mine, as evidenced by how quickly the Federation scum found him.

"Go to Aspar and ask about, and see if there is some clue that will lead us to the SD *Reynolds*. More importantly, I would have you be certain Jora'nal left no way for Reynolds to trace me back to my location. Until I have prepared the fleet, I want no interruptions from upstart pawns."

"Your will is mine, Lord," the Voice replied. "I will report my findings to you as soon as I have answers."

"As I'm sure you understand," Phraim-'Eh warned, "do not fail me, Voice. My patience is thin of late. I will not tolerate any further disappointment."

"I will not fail you, Lord," the Voice assured him.

Phraim-'Eh chuckled and killed the connection, believing such promises out of the hands of such a puny creature as the Voice.

Reynolds had proven to be a worthy foe, defeating his minions time and again and spoiling his every plot to advance his agenda across the galaxy.

That would end now.

No longer would Reynolds be a thorn in Phraim-'Eh's side. Around him, his fleet grew, ship after ship arriving and falling into place alongside the *Godhand*. Soon, his entire armada would be amassed, and he would strike out to find Reynolds and confront the pawn of Bethany Anne and her accursed Federation.

He would wring the life from her sentient machine, and revenge himself upon the foul creatures that inhabited it.

Phraim-'Eh smiled at that thought, pleasure filling him, his blood tingling in his veins.

Calming at the thought, he returned to his seat and settled back to await word from the Voice and for his fleet to be ready.

He would embark on a journey to lay waste to the SD *Reynolds* soon.

Then he would set his sights higher.

He would take the fight to Bethany Anne and assure his godhood for the entire universe to see.

CHAPTER TEN

The crew of the SD *Reynolds* spent the entire day on Grindlevik 3, enjoying the sights of the new society and feasting among the locals.

The experience was so completely different than Jiya had expected that she couldn't stop smiling, even as the crew made ready to depart the planet and return to the *Reynolds*.

L'Willow and L'Sofee saw them to the shuttle, offering them warm hugs and the best of luck for the trials ahead. They knew some of what the crew faced, having spoken about it while they visited, and wished them good fortune in their endeavors before returning to the vehicle to await Gorad.

"It's too bad you must leave so soon, Reynolds," Gorad told the other AI. "This was hardly a visit worth counting."

Reynolds nodded. "I've no wish to bring Phraim-'Eh and his minions down upon you and your people after all the hard work you've put into bettering your world. This is our fight, and it's best if we head off before trouble follows us."

Reynolds held up the computer Jiya had taken off Jora'nal.

"Besides, we have a set of possible targets to look into, thanks to your help," the AI went on, the three of them having hacked the coding and revealed what Jora'nal had been hiding. "I'm looking to take the fight to Phraim-'Eh and finish it. Now, we have a chance to do just that."

"Then I wish you luck, and hope to see you return soon," Gorad said. "You're welcome anytime."

"Thank you for that," Reynolds told him. "That you abide by your word means much to me, Gorad. It will not be forgotten."

"Nor will it be by me," the other AI assured him. "Be safe, Reynolds." He turned to the crew and said his farewells.

Reynolds grinned once they were done and Gorad had returned to his vehicle, departing seconds after.

"Guess our vacation is officially finished," Ka'nak muttered.

"We need to kill this would-be god so we can take a real vacation," Maddox stated as he started up the ramp of the shuttle. "This place will be fantastic once they get that Gate built. I can see it becoming a must-see destination within a few years, tops. I'd love to come back and see how the planet evolves after that."

"Once we take care of Phraim-'Eh, we can," Reynolds said.

"Then let's get to it." Ka'nak laughed. "We haven't even left, and I already want to come back."

The crew boarded the shuttle to greetings by Fulla Hirvin and Vor Gerfur, the two pilots glad to see them again.

It was an interesting change from the last time they'd been there, when the Grindlovians had been polite but hardly friendly or outgoing. Now, they were practically bubbling with the same energy and optimism as the Telluride.

It made Reynolds proud to have had a hand in the new Grindlevik.

The AI watched the planet as they rose into the air and returned to the SD *Reynolds*. The mood of the crew was somber yet determined when they said goodbye to the two Grindlovians and returned to the bridge.

The visit had been a nice distraction, but there was work to be done.

They had a god to kill.

"How'd it go?" XO asked as they returned.

"Looks like Jora'nal was sloppy regarding security protocol," Reynolds answered, grinning. "Once we got past the firewall system, we were able to suss out several possible locations where we might find Phraim-'Eh."

"Not a specific target, though?" Tactical wondered.

"Unfortunately, no," the AI came back. "There is a reference to a home base, Phraim-'Eh's base of operations, but Jora'nal wasn't high enough in the hierarchy to get an invite. He doesn't know where the planet is, or even what system it's in, from the looks of it."

"The other three locations," Geroux took over, "are apparently places Phraim-'Eh frequented recently on something Jora'nal referred to as his *pilgrimage*. Sounds like it's supposed to be some sort of holy journey to shore up and motivate his cultist base, and maybe to recruit more disciples."

"So, he's running around drafting people for his army?" Tactical asked.

"I think that's exactly it," Reynolds agreed. "People apparently come from all over to visit some of these locations and catch a glimpse of their god."

"Goes to show you there are radical extremists everywhere you go," Tactical stated. "Fucking nutjob meatbags."

"Where are we going to first?" XO asked.

"The closest of the three systems is called 'Rolant,' so we might as well visit these fuckers in order," Reynolds replied. "I'm uploading coordinates into the system, so once we're at stations and ready, we can head out and see what we find."

Ria clambered into her seat and settled in, signaling to the AI that she was ready when he was, and he fed the coordinates in.

Asya and Jiya flanked the captain's chair as Reynolds took his seat. Maddox dropped into Tactical's position, earning a grunt from the AI personality, and Ka'nak, Geroux, Takal, San Roche, and L'Eliana left the bridge to go about their duties.

Reynolds gave them time to reach their stations before he addressed the bridge.

"There's no telling what we're walking into, but it's guaranteed to be hostile territory, so I want everyone on their toes and ready. This is the home turf of the cult, and even if Phraim-'Eh isn't there, he's likely to have numerous assets in place."

"No details on that?" XO wondered.

Reynolds shook his head. "Jora'nal was consumed by his duties aboard the *Pillar*. He was a good servant who knew very little, and Phraim-'Eh clearly liked him that way. For obvious reasons, given the coordinates we were able to pick up from scraping his hard drive. All he knew was in basic terms, vague references. If he had deleted his communication logs, there wouldn't have been shit to go on. But he didn't, so…"

"We have his boss," XO finished.

"Well, we have another lead," Reynolds corrected. "There's nothing definitive, since it appears Phraim-'Eh is a hell of a lot smarter than Jora'nal."

"Speaking of the little shit, what are we going to do with him?" Tactical asked. "He's pretty damn useless, especially now that you hacked his computer. Can I strap him to a Pod and use him as target practice?"

Reynolds chuckled. "Not yet. He doesn't know we've broken his system, so he's likely stewing in his thoughts, wondering what the hell he's going to do. So, for now, we let his ass rot in the cell."

"You're no fun," Tactical grumbled.

Reynolds motioned to Ria. "Ensign Alcott, open a Gate and take us to the Rolant System. Sound General Quarters and be ready for anything."

"Yes, Captain," Ria replied, getting to work.

A moment later, a Gate opened before them, and the SD *Reynolds* slipped through it into the unknown system.

There was a flash, and the ship arrived in the Rolant System, the Gate closing behind them.

"Sweep the system and tell me what we're looking at," Reynolds ordered.

"Those coordinates you uploaded brought us in close to a planet, Captain," Maddox reported. "It's inhabited and modern. Getting lots of Kurtherian energy signatures pinging off the tech there."

"We've got three destroyers peeling out of orbit and heading our way," XO called.

"We're being targeted by planetary weapons systems," Jiya added. "Doesn't look like these folks want us here."

The lights on the bridge dimmed, bathing the crew in red as Asya hit the alert. She thankfully silenced the siren before it could rattle their ears.

"We've been identified already," Maddox said. "No hails. These guys know who we are and why we're here."

"Any sign of Phraim-'Eh?" Reynolds asked.

"Negative," Jiya answered. "These look like grunts. He might be on the planet, but I'm not getting the sense that we walked into his hidey-hole. More like a military base of some kind."

Weapons fire hit the gravitic shields as the planetary defense systems engaged, missiles exploding uselessly before reaching the hull.

"Returning fire," Tactical announced.

He launched missiles in return, the screen showing them streaking down through the atmosphere to answer the hostility from below. Sensors picked up flares of anti-aircraft fire looking to counter, and bright flashes of light exploded in missiles' wakes.

"They've got substantial defense weaponry down there," Tactical reported. "We landed a couple of hits, but most of the missiles were shot down."

"Then we'll have to fire more," Reynolds advised.

Tactical laughed. "*Now* you're talking my language."

"Destroyers are on us, Captain," Ria announced.

The SD *Reynolds* shuddered as if on cue.

The destroyers spread out and came at the superdreadnought from different angles, each trying to flank it and avoid coming at the ship head-on.

Reynolds chuckled. "They know about the ESD," he commented. "They're looking to dance around us."

"You blame them?" Jiya asked, grinning.

"No, but it makes them look like chickenshits," Reynolds countered. "Warm up the ESD a little, just enough to make sure they realize we're arming it, Tactical."

"I hope these captains are wearing their brown uniforms today." Tactical would have smirked if he could have. "The ESD is cooking."

"We've got a cruiser rising from the back side of the planet," Asya advised.

"Then let's get these destroyers out of here so we're not playing tag with all of them at once," Reynolds commanded.

The ship trembled as more fire pounded the shields. Ria maneuvered the SD *Reynolds* about to bring the ESD into play...at least as far as the enemy believed.

Reynolds had no intention of firing the weapon and wasting it on the destroyers, but their fear of it offered a perfect tactical diversion. As long as they thought it would be deployed, the captains would be cautious. Reynolds could use that to his advantage.

"You're right," Tactical said a moment later. "The destroyers are turning with us, angling to stay on our flanks and away from our nose."

"Target their likely locations based on our positional shifts, then," Reynolds called. "Let's see if we can't walk them into something."

Reynolds activated the ship's comm and reached out to the inventor. "Takal, I want cloaked mines pumped out to the coordinates I provide."

"On it," Takal came back.

Railgun fire and cannon bursts streaked from the SD *Reynolds* as they turned, and the first of the destroyers moved directly into the deadly hail.

Its shields flared and flickered as Tactical poured it on, backing the onslaught up with missile fire. The enemy seemed to freeze in place, surprised at how easily Tactical had pinpointed their direction of motion, only allowing the assault to cause more damage.

In one aft section, the destroyer's shields buckled and burned out. Railgun fire peppered the hull, spewing debris in a line across the armor. Then the missiles hit.

Explosions ripped across the destroyer's hull, and the sudden volcano of atmosphere spewing from the ship was a clear sign of success.

"Direct hit," Tactical called.

The AI personality targeted the downed shields and hammered the hull. A ripple of energy ran along the armor, splitting the ship in two as the accumulation of damage proved too much for the ship to handle.

A moment later, the destroyer was listing, the remainder of its shields fluttering as they died.

The bridge rumbled as the other destroyers closed, and the planetary weapon systems continued to engage the SD *Reynolds*.

Alarms sounded as the gravitic shields were penetrated in several locations. Sensors showed explosions battering the hull.

"Took a couple of good hits on the starboard flank, but the armor's holding," Jiya reported. "Increasing power to the shields there to compensate."

"Bring us about, Ensign," Reynolds ordered. "Turn that section away from the planet so they can't concentrate on it."

"Aye aye, sir," Ria replied, bringing the SD *Reynolds* about to give the starboard shields time to recover.

Dozens of explosions rippled down the length of one of the remaining destroyers as the SD *Reynolds* repositioned.

"It's like the Fourth of July out there." Reynolds laughed, seeing the explosions come one after another.

The enemy ship veered at the unexpected attack, but the captain's resulting panic walked them into even more danger.

The cloaked mines Takal had spit into space had been more effective than Reynolds could have hoped.

The ship plowed right into the makeshift minefield as it tried to flee the invisible enemy. Explosions rang out all across its nose, the brilliance of them obscuring the front of the destroyer for several seconds.

Tactical unleashed on the ship then, raining railgun fire,

missiles, and blaster fire to take advantage of the weakened shields at the nose of the craft.

A wave of explosions followed, and the destroyer was engulfed, section by section, blowing up and flinging debris everywhere as its final act.

"We're still being pounded by those damn guns on the planet," Maddox reported. "Our return fire is largely being negated by the AA."

"Shifting to targeting the defense outposts," Tactical announced. "We worried about collateral damage?"

"Not here," Reynolds replied. "This is a cult haven and a military outpost, not some compound in the middle of an innocent population. Take these fuckers out."

Tactical chortled. "Carpet-bombing it is."

Although the AI personality had been holding back to avoid wholesale ruin of the planet, he no longer had to worry about it.

A barrage of fire and missiles rained down on the planet in response to the constant fire pounding them from below. Explosions were marked on the viewscreen as Tactical poured it on, overwhelming the AA systems and shredding the planet as if tilling a field.

Zoomed in, the screen showed thousands of explosions moving across the surface of the planet like a tsunami. And one by one, the AA went silent as they were scorched, the tracers in the air slowing from a raging storm to a light drizzle in just seconds.

"Burn, motherfucker, burn!" Tactical laughed as he continued pounding the planet.

"Where's that cruiser?" Reynolds asked, pulling his eyes

from the screen and returning his focus to the battle in space.

"Closing on us, but they're still out of range," Asya replied.

"Then let's deal with this destroyer before it gets here," Reynolds suggested.

More explosions erupted outside as the last of the destroyers came across more of the cloaked mines Takal had laid down for them.

"Excellent work, Takal," Reynolds said over the comm.

"It's easy when they're willing to run right into them," the inventor came back.

"They're giving us their belly." Jiya laughed, motioning to the screen.

Sure enough, the destroyer had rolled, perhaps predicting where the next mines would be laid, in an effort to avoid ripping up their shields against a weapon they couldn't detect.

Tactical, however, knew exactly where the mines were.

"That was kind of smart, in a fucking stupid way," Tactical said, chuckling.

The enemy ship had actually moved in the right direction to avoid running into more of the mines. However, the captain's decision provided the SD *Reynolds* with a better target, and it was the last mistake he would ever make.

Tactical concentrated fire on the field of mines that floated en masse alongside the destroyer's belly. Railgun fire triggered the mines, setting them off and starting a chain reaction of explosions that sliced through the destroyer's shields and rained fire across its armored hull.

The follow-up barrage of fire, with no shields remaining to deflect it, smashed into the destroyer, to great effect.

The warship shuddered as its belly was peeled open. Eviscerated, the ship spewed atmosphere, crew, and debris into space as though its intestines were spilling out.

The hull, unable to maintain integrity, split, tearing the ship in two, almost as if it were a peeled banana. It tore apart lengthwise, pieces of armor and hull behaving like toppling stones, bouncing off the rest of the ship as momentum carried it forward.

So close to orbit, with no engines to redirect it, the planet started pulling it in, and the destroyer began its final flight. Flames flickered, and the ship glowed a brilliant orangish-red as it returned home for the last time.

"Ashes to ashes, and fuck that fuck." Tactical intoned as the enemy ship was devoured by the atmosphere.

"We've got one more to worry about," Reynolds reminded them.

The cruiser moved into range then and began to unleash on the SD *Reynolds*, shaking up the ship and the crew as its fire pounded the gravitic shields.

"Sitrep!" Reynolds ordered as the cruiser engaged.

"Scanners show there are no more ships headed our way anywhere in the system," Jiya replied. "The planetary guns in the eastern hemisphere are still active, but Tactical is steadily blowing the shit out of things in that direction."

"Damn right, I am," Tactical said. "The threat from the planet is negligible at this point, but they're still popping off shots."

"Tactical's efforts have also reduced the local population drastically," Jiya went on. "Their numbers were concentrated around the guns, and there aren't many of those left now."

"That means we'll likely find little intelligence down on the planet," XO advised.

Reynolds shrugged. "The grunts aren't going to have much to tell us anyway, so no loss there," he answered, then pointed at the incoming cruiser. "Those are the bastards we want to get our hands on. Keep bombing the planet and take their base out completely, then ready a boarding team."

The crew acknowledged the orders and got to work as Reynolds examined the fast-approaching cruiser.

"Let's cripple that ship so we can go pay them a visit," he told Tactical.

"Gladly!" the AI personality replied, and Reynolds could practically hear him grinning.

CHAPTER ELEVEN

The enemy cruiser had no intention of going down easy.

It had seen and recognized the tactics deployed by the SD *Reynolds* with the mines, so its first act was to flash the entire field. Tracers of energy brightened the blackness of space, the resulting explosions only adding to the flickering brilliance between the opposing ships.

"I hate when they're smart," Asya said, grunting as the viewscreen adjusted to the brightness outside.

"Just takes a little longer to punch holes in them, that's all," Reynolds countered. "Speaking of which..."

"On it," Tactical replied.

The SD *Reynolds* unloaded on the cruiser as Ria took advantage of the other ship's focus on the mines.

The cruiser's shields sparked as it deflected their efforts, the SD *Reynolds* veering off and peppering the port side of the enemy craft.

The cruiser returned fire, and the bridge trembled under the fierce assault.

"Swing us about and threaten them with the ESD," Reynolds ordered.

The *Reynolds* turned instantly, angling to bring its nose about. The cruiser seemed unimpressed, holding its ground and firing hordes of missiles in return.

XO grunted. "So much for that bluff."

"It's only a bluff if I don't actually pull the trigger," Tactical shot back.

"We can't risk wiping the ship out. We need it in one piece," Reynolds warned. "Kill the ESD and save the energy. We're not going to out-poker-face this captain, obviously."

"ESD down, much to my regret," Tactical reported.

The bridge rattled again as the cruiser continued to pound the SD *Reynolds*. Tactical returned fire as the two ships streaked past each other, each side doing its damndest to take the other out first.

"It's packing more heat than a normal cruiser," Jiya called. "It's not on the level of the *Pillar*, but that cruiser isn't stock. The cult has upgraded it."

As the two ships came about to face each other again, Reynolds examined the ship. The two traded fire, neither side having a distinct advantage at a distance, despite the fact that the SD *Reynolds* packed more firepower.

The enemy's shields had been enhanced similarly to those of the *Pillar*, and it was shrugging off enough of the hits that what little crept past did effectively no damage to the armored hull.

It was as if the two ships were jousting in space, each side's lances clanging off the armor of the other.

On the third pass, seeing the ineffectiveness of their current tactics, Jiya raised her hand.

"We're not in class, First Officer Lemaire." Reynolds smiled. "Just tell me what you're thinking."

"If that's not an invitation to disaster, I don't know what is," Tactical muttered.

"I've got an idea," Jiya said.

"Then spit it out," Reynolds told her.

She did, and the AI chuckled when she finished.

"I used to think that most of you not having had any structured tactical training was a bad thing, but I'm starting to believe it's an advantage," Reynolds said with a grin. "You think up some crazy shit." He motioned to Jiya. "Do it."

"Doing it," she replied, grinning broadly, and triggering the comm to relay her orders.

"Coordinate with Jiya when she's ready, Tactical," Reynolds ordered. "Until then, let's keep this prick occupied so he doesn't suspect anything."

"You don't think their captain isn't contemplating a new way to come at us, the same way we are them?" XO asked.

"Of course they are," the AI answered, "but I can guaran-fucking-tee they'll stick to the handbook until they run out of pages. No one does crazy like the crew of the SD *Reynolds*."

"I'm taking that as a compliment, however you meant it." Asya laughed.

The cruiser came about again, and true to Reynolds' prediction, its only response to the relative stalemate was to come at the SD *Reynolds* from another angle, showing clear signs that it intended to veer suddenly and try to deliver damage while minimizing the amount of return fire it absorbed.

Reynolds told Ria to let it come on. They didn't need to make any radical adjustments to their path for Jiya's plan to play out. They only needed to be close enough to make it a surprise.

"Ready!" Jiya announced. "Launch systems green."

Reynolds acknowledged the statement with a nod, but he held his tongue, waiting for the right moment to launch their plot.

The cruiser streaked toward them, then did as he expected, veering quickly as Tactical engaged it, feinting to avoid return fire as it moved along the starboard side of the SD *Reynolds*.

"Hard to port, Ensign!" Reynolds called.

Ria maneuvered the superdreadnought smoothly, angling off to open up space between the two ships.

"Pods away," Jiya reported.

"Those poor Pods," Tactical commented.

Packed with mines, the trio of cloaked Pods shot free of the hangar bay, which was positioned directly in line with the enemy ship. Piloted remotely by Jiya, they streaked straight at the cruiser in a tight formation before the enemy could slip away.

The shuttles exploded as they collided with the cruiser's shields, a flash of vicious energy erupting before flaring out.

It took out a swath of the enemy ship's shields along with it.

"Now, Tactical!" Reynolds commanded.

"Don't have to tell me twice," Tactical replied as he hammered the hole in the cruiser's shields.

Perfectly placed, the exploding Pods had taken out the cruiser's defenses near its aft end, leaving its engines undefended. Tactical tore it a new ass, a variety of weapons fire battering the back end of the cruiser and wrecking its engines and a large portion of the ship beyond that.

There was a sudden influx of debris clattering across the SD *Reynolds'* shields as they watched the enemy cruiser's engines flare and die.

A quick burst of atmosphere vented from the other side of the engines, but it was almost immediately quelled, showing that the majority of the ship's system were still online.

That was something Reynolds would have to remedy.

"Bring us around and hit it again," the AI ordered. "Be surgical. I want their guns down but their bridge intact."

Tactical laughed. "That's greedy of you."

"Just do it," Reynolds countered as they came back around, easily closing on the wrecked ship.

The cruiser fired all it had to keep the SD *Reynolds* off its back, but it didn't stand a chance. Its blows were deflected by the gravitic shields easily enough.

Tactical took his time and picked at the enemy ship, piecing it up until nothing remained that posed a danger to the superdreadnought.

"Stripped and ready for a cavity search," Tactical announced once he was finished.

"Then let's board her and see what there is to find. Put us in position, Ensign. Tactical, provide distractions with boarding umbilicals to keep them guessing as to where we're really coming in," Reynolds said. "Asya, you have the conn. Maddox and Jiya, you're with me."

The three left the bridge and marched down to the hangar bay, where Ka'nak and Geroux met them.

"We flying in?" the Melowi asked.

"Why not?" Jiya countered. "Their shields are down, their hangar bay is cracked open, and they think we're coming in through the boarding tubes." She ushered Ka'nak into the Pod.

The warrior grunted affirmatively and stomped inside. The others followed, and Jiya brought up the rear. She plopped into the pilot's chair beside Reynolds and waited for the crew to strap in.

Once they had, she triggered the Pod's cloak, eased out of the hangar bay, and started toward the enemy ship. Debris floated around the cruiser, bits and pieces being stirred up by Tactical as he pecked away at the ship with low-powered bursts of fire, further degrading their systems and doing what he could to distract and take out the enemy crew.

Invisible to the enemy sensors, whatever remained active, Jiya piloted the Pod around and easily slipped into the cruiser's hangar. Crew rushed about, preparing their escape shuttles, but it was clear they'd never had to abandon ship before.

The hangar bay was total chaos.

Ships and people were everywhere, automated bots confusing the process as everyone scrambled to flee. It was taking three times the amount of time to get things done than it should have.

"Let's give them something else to worry about,"

Reynolds said with a grin. "Park the Pod over there," he told Jiya, pointing to a position where it would be out of the way but close enough to do what he needed it to.

She did as ordered and the Pod set down quietly, engines stilling unnoticed in the frenzied din.

"Cloak yourselves, and let's go," Reynolds told them.

The crew vanished, leaving nothing but their vague outlines, then exited the Pod and slipped around the far end of the hangar bay, avoiding the clusterfuck.

"We should have just transported in," Ka'nak said. "Feels like a missed opportunity to test the system in a real-world situation."

"We're still not sure if we can cloak in transport or if it disrupts it," Geroux said. "Besides, we don't have a good layout of the cruiser. While they don't have any shields to deflect us, there's still a chance we can beam into a wall or person."

She shuddered at that thought.

"And we wouldn't be able to do this," Reynolds said, grinning wildly.

The Pod ramp retracted, and the hatch closed. The ship's engines started up, then suddenly it was no longer cloaked.

"Uh, what are you doing?" Jiya asked.

"Taking a page out of your tactics book," Reynolds answered.

The Pod shot forward.

The crew in the hangar bay saw it then, the strange ship appearing out of nowhere and shooting straight toward the thickest congregation of them.

Shouts and screams rang out even above the clatter, but those didn't last long.

"We might want to move around the corner," Reynolds suggested as the Pod crashed into the crowd of enemy shuttles and crew.

"Oh, shit!" Jiya smirked as they darted around the corner.

There was a loud crash, then explosions rang out behind them. Reynolds had triggered the Pod's self-destruct system as it collided with the crowd.

The ground trembled under the crew's feet as their ships went up in a chain reaction. The massive door that separated the hallway from the hangar bay slammed shut, alarms whooping overhead. Rattling explosions continued from the other side, only slightly muted by the sealed hatch.

"What the hell are you guys doing over there?" Asya called over the comm.

"Reynolds is renovating the hangar bay," Jiya answered with a barked laugh.

"We're going to need a Pod-printer similar to the aggro-printer if these guys keep this up," Maddox commented. "We're going to run out of Pods."

"Well, I hope it was worth it," Asya went on, "because you've drawn attention to what was supposed to be a quiet entry. Scanners show people headed your way."

"That means there will be fewer on the bridge when we get there," Reynolds replied, shrugging. He waved the crew on.

They jogged down the corridor, stepping to the side and squeezing into doorways or repair alcoves in order to avoid the cultists storming past in search of them.

One of them stumbled over Ka'nak's invisible foot and toppled to the ground at the back of his group. He grunted and clambered to his feet, glancing around to see what happened as his brethren left him behind.

He never did figure it out.

Ka'nak stepped out of his doorway and drove a fist through the cultist's visor. There was a sharp *crash* of plas-glas breaking, then the meatier *crunch* of the cultist's head following suit, and Ka'nak stood there with a helmeted head wrapped about his fist.

He shook his arm, and the body toppled to the deck with a *thump.*

"Stuff him in that alcove so no one spots him right away," Reynolds told the Melowi.

Not that it mattered much. They were nearly to the bridge, and it would be damned obvious that the enemy cruiser had been boarded in a few more minutes.

Ka'nak stashed the body and the crew started off again, reaching the bridge after only having to hide a couple more times.

"Pop the door," Reynolds told Geroux as they arrived.

Geroux got to work, hacking into the simple door-locking mechanism and giving a thumbs-up a second later. "We're good."

Reynolds motioned for them to go and Geroux hit the door, sliding it open. The crew darted inside…

Directly into a group of outgoing cultists.

They slammed into them before there was a chance to realize what was happening and avoid them.

Cultists stumbled backward at the collision, eyes wide, but these people were fanatics. What surprise they suffered was replaced immediately by suspicion and action.

They opened fire at the same time the *Reynolds'* crew did.

Jiya hissed as she was struck in the shoulder. She stumbled backward and edged behind the wall, Geroux at her side.

Reynolds was struck twice, as was Maddox.

The general fell to the deck with a pained groan, facing away from the enemy. Ka'nak positioned himself directly in front of the general and went trigger-free.

The Melowi's vicious attack drove the cultists back into the cover of the bridge. Reynolds joined him, cutting down several of the cultists as they ran. The entire bridge turned on the crew at that point, and the corridor was filled with shrieking death.

Ka'nak grabbed Maddox by the ankle and flung him around, sliding the general into the wall and out of the line of fire. Then the Melowi, shrugging off several more blows, thanks to his armor, leaned out of the way, pressing his back to the wall.

Reynolds stood his ground a moment longer, making the cultists pay for their aggression. It was only when the enemy started to get a bead on him that he pulled back to avoid return fire.

"You okay, Maddox?" Jiya asked, staring at the general, who lay on his back on the other side of the corridor.

"I'm...good," he answered, although it was clear he was breathing heavily.

"Biometrics tell me he'll be fine," Asya reported from the SD *Reynolds*. "Cracked rib, but no internal damage."

"Are my ribs not internal?" Maddox asked, holding his side.

"We can't stay here long," Jiya told the crew. "There's no doubt that the captain has summoned every able body to the bridge to deal with us."

Reynolds agreed. He eased out and sprayed the bridge with covering fire, using his enhanced senses to survey the layout of the stations and the positioning of the remaining cultists.

He didn't like what he saw.

"There are twenty-two cultists packed onto the bridge, the majority of them taking cover behind the command stations," the AI reported.

"Grenade?" Ka'nak asked, holding one up.

"Seeing as how we came here to raid the computer systems for intel, I think a grenade might be overkill, don't you?" Jiya asked.

Ka'nak shrugged. "Maybe just a little."

"No grenades," Reynolds affirmed, not wanting the Melowi to toss the weapon onto the bridge before he could give clear orders not to.

"I've got another way," Geroux said.

She reached into her pouch and pulled out a handful of tiny drones like the ones they'd used in Jora'nal's hideout. The tech activated them, letting them hover in the air around her until they were all ready to go. Then she cupped them back into her hands and threw them into the room.

The drones scattered.

They shot across the bridge, strafing cultists and wreaking havoc everywhere they went.

The cultists, unsure what they were up against, opened fire on the tiny drones to try to take them out. The drones were too fast; they zigged and zagged and hurtled straight at the faces of the cultists, stealing their focus and driving them out of cover in some instances.

"I'm thinking now would be a good time to go inside," Geroux suggested, waving to the bridge door as if she were inviting the crew to dinner.

Ka'nak was the first one inside.

Still cloaked, and having regained the element of surprise, the warrior was on top of the cultists before they realized the drones were nothing more than a distraction.

A deadly one.

Ka'nak angled around the stations to clear his line of fire, and he opened up. Rounds ripped through the unarmored cultists and tore them apart, bodies dropping between the consoles.

Reynolds strode to the opposite side, keeping the angle to avoid friendly fire, and did the same. The cultists pushed toward him by Ka'nak's onslaught ran into Reynolds' barrage.

Geroux and Jiya moved in front of the door and targeted anyone who stepped out from behind cover to shoot or try to escape.

Maddox rolled onto his stomach and kept watch on the corridor at their back while the *Reynolds'* crew made short work of the cultists on the bridge.

A smoky moment later, it was all over.

Jiya ran over and grabbed Maddox and helped him to

his feet. Cultists turned the corner then, and Jiya let off bursts of gunfire to keep them back as she pulled the general onto the bridge and out of the line of fire.

Geroux sealed the bridge and scorched the lock so it wouldn't open.

"We've got a few minutes," the young tech told them, "but not much longer than that."

"Should be all we need," Reynolds answered. He waved Geroux over to him. "Ka'nak, you and Jiya on the door. If the cultists start getting through before we're done, give them hell."

"Yes, sir," Jiya and the Melowi answered in unison as they posted themselves on either side of the bridge door.

"Geroux, hack their databases and get me everything you can," the AI told her.

She nodded and went to work without a word, fingers flying across the keypad of her wrist computer, and then on the ship's console before her.

Reynolds reached out over the comm. "Takal, transport Maddox back to the *Reynolds,* and get him to the infirmary and taken care of."

"I'm fine," the general argued. "I can finish the mission."

"It's not a suggestion," Reynolds clarified. "We're only here for a few minutes longer, and you need that rib looked at to make sure you don't end up with a punctured lung."

Maddox scoffed, then winced, grabbing his side with an annoyed grimace. "Fine."

"Now, Takal," Reynolds said.

The general vanished right after, completely disappearing as if he had never been there to begin with.

"I'm never going to get used to seeing that," Jiya commented. "It's so…weird, people just *poofing* away like that."

"It's a handy transportation method, especially when people keep blowing up the Pods." Ka'nak laughed, casting a sideways glance at Reynolds, then Jiya.

"Probably true." Jiya smiled.

"I'm in," Geroux called. She clattered at the keyboard, then grinned. "All data has been scanned and is being uploaded to the SD *Reynolds'* servers."

There was a loud *boom* at the bridge door as the cultists realized they couldn't bypass the wrecked lock and they needed to be more creative to get inside. The floor and walls shuddered in response to the blow they'd delivered.

"How much longer?" Reynolds asked Geroux.

"All done," she answered after a short pause. She disengaged her system from the ship's and spun on a heel. "We're good to go."

"I'd love to see the faces of the cultists when they get in here and realize we're gone. Vanished without a trace," Jiya said, her smile infectious.

"Trigger the flux capacitor, Doc!" Reynolds called over the comm.

There was no response.

"Uncultured swine," Reynolds barked, shaking his head. "Transport us out of here, Takal."

That time, the inventor complied, and the crew was teleported back to the bridge of the SD *Reynolds*, leaving the cruiser behind.

Reynolds motioned to Tactical as soon as they arrived. "Put that hunk out of its misery."

Tactical did exactly that, blowing the ship to pieces and letting its remains drift quietly into the void of space.

"What now?" XO asked.

"We scrape the cruiser's databases and see what we can find," Reynolds answered. "Between it and what we've grabbed from Jora'nal's computer, maybe we'll have a better lock on where our supposed god is hiding out."

"Until then?" Jiya asked.

Reynolds grinned wide and turned to face her. "How would you like to go home?

CHAPTER TWELVE

The Voice arrived on Aspar, to learn that what he'd been told was only part of the story.

It hadn't been the Federation crew who'd brought about Jora'nal's death and the destruction of the cult's place on the planet, but Jora'nal himself.

The Voice growled when he learned that, wondering if his master already knew what had happened. What would he tell him now?

That their own disciple had been the cause of losing both the SD *Reynolds* and their foothold on the planet?

He didn't look forward to speaking with his lord again, but it would happen soon whether he wanted to or not.

First, however, he would learn all he could about what transpired here on Aspar before he reached out to Phraim-'Eh.

The Voice drew in a slow, deep breath and let it linger in his lungs until the char began to burn. Then he let it out, staring down the destruction left behind by Jora'nal.

"Fool," he mocked the disciple in absentia. "You deserved worse."

The Voice marched over the wreckage, grateful that the powers that be of Asparian society cared little about the execution of law and order. Jora'nal's death had been justice as far as they were concerned.

The loss of the cult's headquarters and disciples and resources here mattered little to the ruling elite of Aspar. They only cared that it wouldn't happen again, so they had banned the cult from settling again or rebuilding in the wake of the catastrophe.

Phraim-'Eh would not appreciate that, and the Voice was sure his master would rain down judgment upon the rulers of Aspar, but it likely wouldn't be soon.

The Voice's master was consumed with destroying the Federation spawn of Bethany Anne, the AI superdreadnought who had wrought such harm to his plans of expansion.

No, Phraim-'Eh would chase the sentient ship to the ends of the universe before he calmed enough to deal retribution for such petty grievances as Aspar evicting them.

But when he did return, the elite of Aspar would rue their decision. They'd be so much ash, such as what the Voice trod upon now. There would be no mercy or compassion shown in Phraim-'Eh's vengeance.

The Voice thrilled at the idea, imagining what his master would do to exact his revenge.

He only prayed he remained alive to witness it.

As things were, there was little hope of that.

The Voice traversed the scorched blocks that had been part of a city until just recently, and he came upon the blast point where Jora'nal had made his final ill-advised stand against the Federation agents.

There'd been no word as to their condition, but common sense told the Voice that Reynolds and his people had survived the blast or the SD *Reynolds* would have remained nearby to deal with such a tragic loss.

The timeline the locals had given him largely confirmed that.

The explosion here on the planet had occurred first, followed by the destruction of the *Pillar* in space. That made him think Reynolds and the others had slipped away without issue, though given the ruin of the neighborhood, he couldn't imagine how they'd managed that.

Nothing sentient could have survived a blast like the one that had occurred there.

"But if something did, there has to be a trace of it. A hint," the Voice said to himself as he clambered over a short stretch of wall and entered what had once been a building that had housed the local cult members. "Maybe I'll find the android's skull to parade before the master."

He laughed at that, given how unlikely it was.

Reynolds had proven himself durable and quite resilient, much to the Voice's regret.

"This would all be so much easier if you would just die, android!" he shouted to the empty, smoke-shrouded sky. "Why can't you just *die*?"

The Voice examined the blast site, scanning it for residual energies. He didn't expect to find anything, but when he picked up the barest of blips of current still active in the area, he was surprised.

He followed the line of the signal out of the destroyed building, realizing once he was about two blocks to the east of the explosion that the damage there was far less traumatic.

He circled a half-demolished building, tracing the signal to a smaller, squat building another block farther that looked almost whole.

Its neighbor had apparently protected it behind its bulk, taking the blow and leaving the smaller building sheltered in its lee.

The Voice went to the building and slipped inside.

It was little better than the other wrecks, but it was whole.

He traced the signal to a darkened corner covered by debris. With eager hands, he knelt and cast the trash and wreckage aside and ducked into the corner, looking for the source of the signal.

He'd already figured out what it was by then, but he was glad to see the tiny box screwed to the wall, a single green light beeping on its face, glowing eerily in the dust.

It was Jora'nal's backup server, which he used to send coded messages to the Voice and their master from inside the signal-blocked headquarters.

It was still operational.

The Voice wiped the dust off and synced his computer to the server, downloading its contents. So little on it, the process only took a few seconds before it was complete.

The Voice rose from his knees, dusted them off, and

commanded his computer to display the contents of the rescued server.

"Please don't let him be a greater fool than I already believe," the Voice muttered as the information scrolled across the screen.

A moment later, the Voice groaned, realizing Jora'nal was every bit the fool he'd prayed he wasn't.

There, amidst the various information the disciple kept, were his communication logs, each time-stamped and encoded with delivery information.

"Damn you, Jora'nal!" the Voice shrieked, slamming a fist into the wall and kicking up a cloud of gray dust and debris. Shards of stone pattered to the ground around his feet.

Although the information was insufficient at face value to lead the Federation to Phraim-'Eh, he knew there was enough for an AI to trace back and eventually find the master.

There was no doubt about that.

"You've damned us all, Jora'nal," the Voice called. "I pray your death was painful."

The Voice knew there was no chance of that.

Jora'nal had been granted mercy in the form of a quick death. Now it would be the Voice who suffered for his failure to keep their intelligence secure.

Nothing left to do, the Voice activated his comm and reached out to his master.

If death is coming, I'd rather not wait, he thought, although he couldn't keep his hands from trembling.

When the channel was opened on the other end and

Phraim-'Eh was reached and put on the line, the Voice had summoned what was left of his courage.

"Jora'nal has betrayed us, Master," he said.

The declaration was greeted with brooding silence.

"Although there is no sign of his remains or those of the Federation scum, I found the server for the headquarters he maintained here."

The Voice paused to catch his breath before continuing.

"On it are coordinates that will lead the SD *Reynolds* to several locations of strategic value to you, Lord."

"Let me guess," Phraim-'Eh interrupted, the words spilling loose as though he were a serpent. "One of those locations is the military base on Rolant?"

"Yes, Master," the Voice answered meekly.

He knows.

It was clear how he did, too.

"Reynolds has already been there?" he asked, knowing the answer.

"He has," Phraim-'Eh replied, "and left it a smoldering ruin. Three destroyers and a cruiser were destroyed there, too, and countless disciples left to bleed out in the sand."

His master's voice grew sharper and more jagged with every passing moment.

"With no witnesses alive to inform me of what happened, I have to assume that Reynolds was able to scrape the databases of the ships and, judging by Jora'nal's example, I can only presume there is information there that should not be. Information that might lead them to my holdings, beyond what he already possesses."

The Voice swallowed hard as the understanding of what his master was saying began to dawn on him.

Even if they captured or killed Reynolds and his people, the information he held would be sufficient to find Phraim-'Eh and all of his installations. Were the android to forward this intelligence to Bethany Anne or anyone else at the Federation, there would be no end to the hell that would be visited upon them.

Phraim-'Eh was not ready to face the entire might of the Federation yet, regardless of how powerful he might be.

Were Bethany Anne to arrive at the head of her full might, the Cult of Phraim-'Eh would be nothing more than a minor footnote in the annals of history.

Reynolds needed to be stopped before that happened.

"I will follow their trail, Master," the Voice promised. "And I will reach out to the other installations and prepare them before the SD *Reynolds* arrives. I'll have them vacate and leave nothing behind for the scum to find."

"I have already contacted the Suri and Hajh installations and warned them of Reynolds' coming, but dependent upon which one they go to first, there is little we can do. Hajh is barely more than a forward operating outpost in the middle of a frostbitten planet. They will offer Reynolds no resistance.

"As such, I will travel there and hope to reach it before the Federation scum arrive. You travel to Suri and help prepare their evacuation. I want nothing left behind to further the Federation's intelligence, is that clear?"

"It is, Master," the Voice answered reverently.

"I had not expected to have to chase this android when I vowed to take the fight to him, but I will do what I must to tear his star from my sky," Phraim-'Eh vowed. "Contact me once you've arrived on Suri."

The connection died without another word, and the Voice let out the breath he'd been holding during the entire conversation. His shoulders slumped, and he groaned as the weight of what was transpiring settled over him.

The end was coming, one way or another.

He prayed to be on the winning side.

CHAPTER THIRTEEN

The planet Lariest appeared on the screen as the SD *Reynolds* Gated into Jiya's home system.

It was Geroux, Takal, and Maddox's home, too.

The brilliant blues and greens gave her pause as she looked down upon her former home, still amazed by how beautiful it looked from up here. It had been a long time since she'd been there last, or so it felt.

Geroux came over and took her hand as they stood at the viewport, and even Maddox seemed to shuffle about in his seat at the sight.

"It's beautiful, isn't it?" Geroux asked.

Jiya nodded. "From up here," she replied, the realization of what they'd left behind washing over her then.

It hadn't been a friendly or fond farewell when they'd left, and Jiya wondered what kind of reception they'd garner now that they had returned.

She wouldn't have long to wonder.

"We're being hailed by the planet, Captain," Comm announced.

"Haven't seen that happen before," Maddox said from his station, the Pod-doc having already repaired his injured rib. Dr. Reynolds had signed off for him to return to his duty station.

Jiya agreed.

The Larians weren't known for their strong orbital defense, and she was just as surprised by the greeting as Maddox was.

"Onscreen," Reynolds ordered.

If he thought the message was strange, he didn't show it.

A no-nonsense face appeared on the viewscreen. Her reddish skin glistened under the lights, and her dark hair was pulled into a tight tail behind her head. Black eyes stared across the void, and Jiya felt a sudden pang of homesickness at seeing someone contacting them from her former home.

"I am Paltrus Varl of the Lariest Space Defense Initiative. You are entering Lariest Provincial Space. Please identify yourself and your intent," the soldier said in an officious voice.

Jiya glanced back at Maddox. "That's new, too," she mouthed.

The general nodded his agreement.

"I am Captain Reynolds of the Federation Superdreadnought *Reynolds*," the AI replied. "For what nation do you speak: the Toller, Marianas, or Melowi?" he asked.

A sly smile cracked the face of the female before it disappeared. "I speak for all of them, Captain Reynolds. Much has changed since your departure from our world."

"So it would seem," Reynolds answered.

"Might I ask if Jiya Lemaire is still a member of your crew?" Paltrus went on. "Is she with you?"

"She is indeed," the AI answered. He glanced at Jiya.

She shrugged, just as surprised as he was at the mention of her name.

At that, Paltrus smiled without hesitation. "Excellent. Her family will be glad to hear it. Please, follow our coordinate prompts to the Marianas Spaceport, and you will be met by transportation to the Provincial palace. We welcome you to Lariest."

The female closed the link as the coordinates were fed to Ria for the ship's landing.

"That was fucking weird," Jiya muttered, looking at Geroux and Maddox.

"I expected a less hospitable welcome from Marianas, I have to admit," Reynolds said.

"You and us both," Maddox agreed, gesturing to indicate him and Jiya. "None of us exactly left on great terms."

"Maybe your father has had a change of heart," Geroux suggested.

Both Jiya and Maddox chuckled at that.

"When groths fly," Jiya joked. "I can't see my father welcoming me back unless he plans to snatch me up and stuff me in a cell for the rest of my days."

"Right alongside me," Maddox said. "This is strange."

"Regardless," Reynolds told them, "we'll be prepared for anything stupid President Lemaire might attempt while we're here. For now, let's just go along with it and see how everything plays out. We saw some pretty amazing changes back on Grindlevik 3, so who knows what's happened? The universe doesn't stop trucking along while we're off gallivanting."

Jiya nodded her agreement. She wasn't the same kid who'd run away from her father time after time, finally landing on the SD *Reynolds* and exploring space. She was herself now, her true self, and nothing her father could do could bring her down.

At least she'd get to see her sisters Reea and Lory again.

A thrill ran through her at that thought.

It had been forever since she'd seen the girls, and Jiya wondered what they'd been up to in her absence.

Worry briefly clouded her mind as she thought of their relationship with their father, but it passed quickly. Her father would never hurt the girls, even if he kept them locked in the palace.

They were safe and taken care of, even if they weren't loved by him.

"Bringing the ship in now," Ria announced as she angled the SD *Reynolds* in preparation to land.

The familiar port sat below them, and Jiya smiled as she recalled her first meeting with Reynolds.

"Hey, look, this is right where you kidnapped me and took me hostage," Jiya said, grinning broadly.

"Hey!" Reynolds argued. "It all worked out in the end, so no harm, no foul."

"For the record, I was against all that," Tactical clarified. "He wanted a crew, but I tried to convince him it was a bad idea. We didn't need any stinking meatbags."

"You'd miss us if we were gone," Jiya told the AI personality.

"You severely overestimate my ability to process fucks," Tactical replied.

Jiya chuckled. "Yeah, I probably do. But if nothing else, I'd miss you," she told him.

Tactical grunted.

"I'd miss you most of all, Scarecrow," Reynolds told her, shooing her from the bridge. "Now get the fuck down to the hangar bay so we can find out what the hell has gone on here in our absence."

Jiya grinned and fired a salute his way. "Yes, sir!"

Jiya grabbed Geroux's hand and led her off the bridge. Maddox clopped along at their heels, while Reynolds called for Ka'nak and Takal to join them.

A hoverlimo met them at the ramp. It pulled up smoothly as they debarked, and the driver climbed out of his seat and opened the back doors for the crew to enter.

"This is a fancy ride to the gallows," Maddox joked. "Classy."

The crew climbed in and the driver started off, weaving and winding through the spaceport traffic on the way toward the palace.

Jiya leaned over the separator between them and the driver and asked, "Are you taking us to see President Lemaire?"

The driver chuckled. "I'm afraid I'm sworn to let the provincial representatives answer all your questions, Ms. Lemaire."

"There's that word again," Maddox said, referring to "provincial." "It seems a rather broad term for Marianas, I'm thinking."

"I agree," Jiya said, sitting back once she realized the

driver intended to stay true to his word and not answer her questions.

Fortunately, it wasn't a long ride to the palace.

They arrived a short while later and were let inside the gates without even having to stop. Not long after, they pulled up to the entryway to the presidential compound and the driver hopped out, opening their doors again.

The crew climbed out a bit hesitantly, still unsure of what was going on.

"All the tension might well drive me to drink," Takal said with a grin, catching Geroux's eyes as he spoke.

For once, she didn't chastise him. "I just might join you, Uncle," she replied with a laugh.

They entangled their arms and marched along the walkway toward the entrance. A suited male greeted them at the door. It wasn't Gal Dorant, the head of Security and personal advisor to her father, whom Jiya had expected. She was pleasantly surprised to not see him.

The old head of security had always bothered her, appearing as though he were crafted from scorched, weathered matchsticks and threaded into an expensive suit.

Instead, there was a young male standing there, his short-cropped hair and brilliant crimson skin making Jiya's look muted in comparison. His eyes were giant pools of obsidian.

He bowed to them. "I am Bal Huro, head of Security for the provincial palace. Please, come inside. Your presence is expected."

Before Jiya could ask Huro anything, he spun on a heel and started off, leading the crew inside.

Memories washed over Jiya as they entered the palace and her eyes wandered everywhere, her head on a swivel.

The first thing that stood out to her was how...*bright* the place appeared.

She remembered it being dark and utilitarian, a reflection of her father's attitude. No lights that weren't absolutely necessary were ever allowed on, and there was no clutter or decorative nuances to make the palace seem like a home to three little girls.

No, it had always been a palace; a place of business for her father.

Now, however, there was a welcomeness to it that had never been there before. Art adorned the walls—historical pieces as well as banners.

It was nothing like the gaudy efforts of the Telluride in their original homes, but there was a comfortable, relaxed feel to the decorations. Whoever had hung them hadn't meant the place to be for stuffy royals or executives only. They had meant for it to bring joy and happiness to those who spent more time there than a quick, formal meeting.

Jiya's first thought was that her father must have died.

It was an awkward thought that she didn't know how to process, but it faded as Bal Huro led them into the throne room.

Jiya's eyes went wide at seeing her young sisters seated side by side in small, simple thrones atop the royal dais.

Despite the time between, she recognized them immediately.

It was Reea and Lory.

Jiya gasped and ran across the throne room. Security shifted around the room to deflect her, but the sisters waved them off and ran down the steps to greet their long-lost sibling.

The three collided in a mass of hugs and kisses and muffled greetings.

"I'm guessing that means we're not here to be executed," Ka'nak stated, grinning. He wiped the back of his hand across his brow. "Whew."

Maddox chuckled. "It would have been just one more chance for you to get into a fight."

The Melowi shrugged. "True."

The sisters called Geroux over, and she joined the melee until the four of them had worn themselves out.

Finally, the two younger sisters composed themselves and returned to their thrones. Bal Huro gathered the crew all together and led them to the foot of the dais. There were smiles all around.

"While introductions are likely unnecessary, it is my duty, regardless," Bal stated. "My ladies, Queens Reea and Lory Lemaire, may I introduce the Federation's Captain Reynolds and his crew, Ka'nak, General Maddox, as I'm sure you remember, Geroux and Takal Durbin and, of course, your sister."

"Queens?" Jiya asked, taken aback by the twin titles. She asked the question that had been nagging her since she realized her father was no longer in charge. "Is father...dead?"

Reea and Lory grinned.

"No, but he likely wishes he was," Reea replied. "He's been imprisoned and will probably spend the remainder of his life there."

"It's hardly a punishment, given how posh his quarters

are, but I'm sure he doesn't see it that way," Lory added.

"What I wouldn't have given for a posh jail when Lemaire imprisoned me," Maddox opined, grinning.

"He's been jailed?" Jiya asked. "Why?"

She realized the question was pretty stupid right after she asked it.

"I mean, besides him being an asshole," she corrected.

"Good thing that's not a jailable offense or I'd be fucked." Reynolds laughed.

"Oh, it's much more than that," Reea assured. "He'd been poisoning the other countries against each other, working behind their backs to bring each of them to each other's throats. War nearly broke out before it was determined what he'd done."

"The war would have broken the whole planet," Lory continued. "But when he was found out, members of the council loyal to our family helped us take control of Marianas. We staged a coup and deposed Father. Then, after we began talks with the Toller and Melowi nations, it was decided that all three of us should join forces for the betterment of the planet."

"We became the Lariest Provincial as a whole, and Lory and I were placed in charge of it all," Reea told them. "Well, sort of." She laughed. "We represent Marianas and the other two nations to visitors to our world, but the Toller and Melowi nations largely manage their own internal issues, as we do with Marianas."

"Still, it is a world away from where the politics of the planet stood when you left to join Captain Reynolds here," Reea said, smiling at her sister.

"And though Father never wanted you to return, know

that you are always welcome here, sister. We've missed you," Lory told her.

"And Captain Reynolds and the crew of the SD *Reynolds* are also always welcome here. The terms agreed upon by President Alac Sumor of the Melowi and President Corrh V'ariat of the Toller regarding your safe passage and supplies anytime you are in the system are in place here in Marianas, too," Reea assured.

"Good to know," Reynolds replied. "We thank you."

The sisters rose and came down the stairs to stand among the crew.

"Now, we know you didn't come all this way simply to catch up, so is there something we can help you with?" Reea asked.

Jiya grinned. "You always were smart girls," she told her sisters. "Better suited for all this than I would ever be."

"A life of adventure suits you, Jiya," Lory told her, smiling pleasantly. "But yes, please tell us what we can do for you."

"We're actually on a mission," Jiya explained. "We needed someplace to bide our time and effect minor repairs to our ship. We only need a place to stay for tonight, where we can catch our breath far from the trials of our mission. We'll be gone again tomorrow."

"Ohh, I wish you could stay longer, Jiya," Reea said, "but we understand. Of course, we have plenty of room for all of you. We can feed you and give you comfortable quarters for the night, or for however long you stay."

"You had me at food, Your Majesties," Ka'nak said with a grin.

Reea and Lory smiled back at him.

"Bal, show our guests to comfortable quarters and provide them with every luxury while they're here," Reea said, waving the head of Security over.

The sisters turned back to Jiya and hugged her.

"We'll let you go about your work, but we'll stop by later and reminisce, if you're okay with that?" Lory asked.

"Of course," Jiya replied. "I want to spend as much time as possible with you. Then, maybe when all this is over, I can come back for a real visit."

"That would be delightful," Reea and Lory said in unison.

The crew said their farewells, and Bal Huro led them out of the throne room and back into the familiar palace. He took them to quarters Jiya remembered as being stuffy and cold, and she realized they had been revamped, much like the rest of the palace.

The suite of rooms was warm and welcoming, and every convenience was made available to them. Bal Huro left them to their own devices shortly after he made sure they were fed appropriately.

The crew sat around eating until they were full.

No matter how great the food the aggro-printers provided was, it was always great to have a home-cooked meal made by someone else.

Reynolds set Jora'nal's stolen computer on the table once it had been cleared. The *thump* of it nudged Jiya out of her pleasant reverie.

"We've got a decision to make," the AI stated. "The information we obtained from the cruiser's databases confirm the locations and nature of the other two places we learned of from Jora'nal's intel. Plus, it hints at several other locations of underground cult activity across the universe. However, none of it points directly to Phraim-'Eh."

"What do we have?" Maddox asked.

"I think we can discount the other locations we've dug up for now, since intel informs us that they are all on densely populated planets not under the cult's control. I find it hard to believe that Phraim-'Eh could hide his flamboyant need to call himself a god without there being some sort of uproar regarding it. Recent news from these locations shows nothing of that sort."

"So, what do we know about the other two spots?" Maddox asked.

"Both locations are military outposts, from what I can garner. One's seriously remote, some frozen planet that goes by the designation of Hajh. There's little information regarding it, beyond that it appears to be some kind of staging outpost. It's intentionally way the hell out there, from the looks of it."

"The other location is called Suri," Geroux added.

Reynolds nodded. "This one seems to be larger and more active cult-wise, but it'll be more like the one at Rolant. It'll be a fight on its own, even if Phraim-'Eh isn't there."

"The latter is more likely to have intel, though," Maddox stated, rubbing his chin. "A staging base at the butthole end of the universe isn't likely to serve much purpose beyond giving the cult's ships one last stopover before they fly out of the galaxy."

"Maybe, but Jora'nal's logs show Phraim-'Eh frequented the place for some reason," Reynolds said. "That makes me think it has more importance than we're being led to believe."

"Where better to hide out than the middle of nowhere?" Jiya asked rhetorically.

"My point exactly," Reynolds agreed.

"Could be what Phraim-'Eh is hoping we'll think," Ka'nak pondered.

"Normally, I'd agree with you, Ka'nak, but I think Jora'nal fucked up when he let us get our hands on his computer. He looked about ready to shit himself when he realized it had survived the explosion. I don't take him for being a good actor. This was intel we weren't supposed to get our hands on. It's probably the same for the cruiser's data, although that seems more benign at first glance."

"Well, what else do we have to do besides tear down Phraim-'Eh's world one brick at a time?" Jiya asked. "I say we hit the out-of-the-way post and see what we find, then go from there. Does it really matter which one we take out first?"

"It might," Reynolds stated. "We could be in for one hell of a fight if word gets out that we're attacking his installations. Shit, they might already know we've gained some sort of intel, and likely know what it is, given what happened on Aspar. They have to suspect that Jora'nal is in our possession by now, even if they don't actually know it."

"Sounds like we've made our choice," Ka'nak said. He grunted, leaning back in his seat, and rubbing his belly. "As such, I say we relax and enjoy the rest of our stay in this comfy palace and make the most of it."

"You know, you actually make sense sometimes, Ka'nak," Maddox told him, raising his glass in a toast.

"*Sometimes,*" Jiya agreed. The crew clinked glasses to that and settled in to plan the specifics of their next move.

CHAPTER FOURTEEN

The night came and went far faster than Jiya wanted it to.

She'd spent time with her sisters, but once she'd returned to the SD *Reynolds*, it was clear it hadn't been enough to satisfy her longing for their company.

She had promised to return when she could, and she meant it, wanting nothing more than watch her sisters grow into the people they'd soon become, but she still had a mission to attend to.

She was part of the crew of the SD *Reynolds*, and that was not only a job she took seriously, but it was an honor. Jiya loved being aboard the ship, traveling across the universe and helping better it one planet at a time.

When they took out Phraim-'Eh, it would release millions of souls from his sway, and she could think of no greater use of her time and efforts.

She stared out as the brilliant orb of Lariest disappeared behind them. Ria guided them into space, readying to Gate them to the outpost Hajh.

Jiya didn't know what they'd find there, but she hoped

it would be Phraim-'Eh himself so they could end this farce of his godhood and put him away. He'd been a shadow at their backs since the moment she'd joined the crew, even if she hadn't known it then.

She'd become a part of Reynolds' mission to destroy Kurtherians, and though Phraim-'Eh wasn't exactly that—a foul descendant of that other vile race—she wanted to help Reynolds lay waste to the person who claimed to be a deity.

"Opening the Gate to the coordinates for Hajh," Ria reported. "Shields and weapons up and at the ready, and scanners set to sweep. Ready to go on your command."

"Do it!" Reynolds told the ensign.

The SD *Reynolds* Gated without hesitation, appearing in the distant galaxy hidden away from the rest of the universe.

Jiya didn't know what to expect when they arrived, but it was every bit as barren and desolate as she'd expected.

"Report," Reynolds called.

"That's one frosty ball out there," Tactical said.

"He's not really wrong." Maddox chuckled. "The temperature is tolerable, but we're looking at it being about negative twenty degrees Celsius on the more habitable side of the planet. Looks to be about negative eighty on the dark side."

"Come to the Dark Side," Tactical muttered. "We have cookies."

"Medicated ones, hopefully," Jiya fired back.

"Scanners show there is an outpost located exactly where Jora'nal's intel shows it to be, and there are maybe two hundred lifeforms packed into it," Ria reported.

"They've pinged us and know we're here, but I'm not picking up any ships anywhere in the area. It looks like they're all alone down there."

"Could be a trap," Asya said, examining the data.

"Could be, but I'm not seeing that they have the resources to surprise us with anything," Reynolds noted.

He double-checked the reports, confirming the ensign's assessment of there being no ships nearby. And with no other planets in the system, the only way someone could reach them quickly enough to cause them grief would be to Gate in.

"I say we pop dirtside and see what we can find," the AI suggested. He looked at Ensign Alcott. "Can you get a clear scan of that outpost and determine a clear layout?"

"Yes, sir," Ria replied, turning to focus on her console.

"Thinking about transporting down?" Maddox asked. "That'll save some wear and tear on the Pods." He laughed.

"We also need more practice with transporting, and this seems like a good time to get that in," the AI replied.

Jiya shrugged. "What the hell. I'm in."

"Besides, it gives us the advantage of surprise, since there's no way they'll expect us to teleport down," Reynolds went on. "They'll be waiting for a Pod or for us to bring the superdreadnought into the atmosphere. As long as we don't do either of those, we'll keep them guessing as to what is going on."

"I've scanned the entire outpost and have a basic map of it," Ria reported. "Since the compound isn't shielded, I was able to do it easily enough. It's a live recording, so it should update to show you where the cultists currently are."

"Excellent. Transfer it to Takal, and have him adjust the

beam for a location nearest what might be the administration section of the compound, and where there is the fewest number of people," Reynolds told her. "We're going to test the accuracy of this system."

"Information transferred," Ria said.

"I've got it plugged in, and we're ready to go, Captain," Takal reported. "I believe I have a suitable location, although it's not directly into the administration area since that section is far too populated to risk transporting you into. All it would take was for a person to slow down, and we might end up merging you with them."

"Fair enough," the AI confirmed. "You've got the conn, Asya. Takal, transport only me down there right now, and I'll survey the location and confirm when it's best to send the rest of the crew."

Ka'nak chuckled. "You just want to go it alone, huh, Captain?"

"You found me out, Ka'nak," Reynolds joked. "Transport me, Takal." He cloaked himself.

Seconds later, the bridge disappeared and Reynolds arrived on the planet, exactly where Takal had intended to send him.

I love this system!

Reynolds glanced around, surveying the landing spot and comparing it against the electronic map Ria had created. It was a perfect match.

Even better, the map continued to function, showing Reynolds where every cultist was in the outpost.

If only it were always this easy, he thought.

He triggered his comm and called up for the rest of the crew. Jiya, Ka'nak, and Maddox appeared beside him moments later, nothing more than hazy outlines picked up by his enhanced senses tuned to identify them in their cloaked state.

"Nice landing," Jiya quipped. "Now, what are we looking for?"

"Anything that points to where Phraim-'Eh might be hiding out," Reynolds replied. "We'll go from here, and make our way to the administration section, taking out anyone who gets in the way."

The crew acknowledged the order and started off behind the android AI.

They made it through several winding corridors before running into anyone. Fortunately, they'd had a heads-up on their arrival.

Two cultists strolled straight toward them through the corridor. Ka'nak and Reynolds moved to either side, pressed against the walls, and waited. When the cultists drew close, Reynolds and Ka'nak reached out and snapped the disciples' necks.

They died without a sound or even realizing what had happened.

The crew stuffed the bodies out of sight down a corridor that showed no cultists nearby, and they moved on.

Down another corridor, a short distance from what they assessed was the administration section, they came upon four cultists standing guard in the hall outside a door.

"We do this quietly or out in the open?" Maddox asked over the private comm, knowing his voice wouldn't carry outside of his helmet as the crew lurked around the corner.

"No point making a mess so soon," Reynolds answered. "Each of us picks a target, and we take them out quietly, no muss, no fuss."

"Roger that," Jiya replied, and Maddox and Ka'nak nodded agreement.

They were on their way a moment later.

The crew eased up in front of the cultists, who were chatting back and forth.

Reynolds grinned as he stood there, ready to end the life of the person before him who couldn't even see him coming.

It wasn't very sporting, and normally Reynolds would hesitate to be so callous, but the cultists had proven they didn't give a damn about morals or the well-being of anyone else besides themselves.

Besides, Reynolds had inherited Bethany Anne's sense of judgment, and that left these cultists, even friendly, chatty ones, wanting.

He glanced at the others, and the crew coordinated their attacks. Then he gave the signal, and they launched into motion.

Four bodies fell as one without a fight, helped to crumple silently to the floor.

Reynolds was about to congratulate the crew when another cultist turned the corner and spotted the four bodies slumped outside the door.

"They're here!" he screamed. "Intruders!"

"Oh, shut the fuck up," Reynolds told the cultist, removing his cloak and blowing his head off.

"So much for stealth." Ka'nak chuckled, turning to cover the door to the administration section, expecting it to come flying open.

Alarms rang out, bathing the corridor in crimson lights.

"You stirred up the hornet's nest," Asya reported from her post aboard the SD *Reynolds*. "Pretty much everyone in the compound is headed your way. I'm updating your maps. Seems there was a slight lag in them, thanks to the transport system."

"Sorry, guys!" Ria called over the comm.

"Geroux and I are adjusting the latency of the system on our end," Takal reported. "Seems there is a bit of lag between systems when you're transported. Hadn't noticed it before because your suits always caught up before you checked the systems."

"Good to know," Reynolds replied, raising his pistol and firing down the hall as one of the red dots on his map appeared.

A cultist shrieked and slammed into the wall behind him, his head a smoldering ruin.

"Seems to be synced up again," the AI reported.

He fired a couple more shots at cultists who stepped out into the corridor, dropping them alongside their head-less companion. The rest of the cultists wised up and stayed behind the cover of the wall.

"They're massing on the other side of the door here," Jiya informed. "Looks like fifteen arranged to cover every angle once the door opens."

"Now would be a good time for a grenade," Ka'nak said, grinning.

"It's always a good time for a grenade with you," Maddox told the Melowi.

"Hey, don't mess with what works," Ka'nak fired back.

"No grenades for you," Jiya told him, waggling a finger his direction.

"Awww, *Mom!*" the Melowi whined, sniggering a second later.

The door started to slide open right then.

It was about halfway when the first barrage of fire exploded out from the inside.

The crew hunkered down, pressing against the walls, but it would only be a second or two more before the door opened wide enough to expose all of them to the cultists' shots.

"Grenade!" Ka'nak screamed, using his helmet to amplify his shout.

His voice reverberated through the corridor as if he'd used a loudspeaker.

"Oh, fuck!" Jiya growled. "You better not—"

She watched as Ka'nak stepped forward and threw something into the crowd of cultists on the other side of the door.

"You didn't?" She started to groan when she realized what he had tossed into the room.

It was his pistol.

The unarmored and unprepared cultists, however, didn't realize that.

They scattered and retreated into the room in a frenzy of assholes and elbows, desperately trying to put something solid between them and the grenade as it *thunked* loudly to the floor.

"Seriously?" Jiya asked the Melowi. "You threw your *gun?*"

Ka'nak shrugged and bolted into the room. "They didn't

know that." He scooped up his weapon and turned it on the fleeing cultists, who were only then realizing that nothing had exploded at their backs.

By then, many of their heads actually *were* exploding, only adding to the confusion.

Ka'nak blasted the cultists from behind, plowing through half of them before the others managed to recover and spin around to attempt a panicked defense.

Jiya joined him at that point.

She sprayed the room, being careful not to hit anything crucial that might contain the information they needed to track down Phraim-'Eh.

Maddox joined them, sniping cultists who'd avoided slaughter and found the wits to return fire.

Seconds later, all the cultists in the room were dead or incapacitated.

Reynolds stepped into the room, firing down the hall to keep the remaining cultists at bay. Ka'nak joined him on the near side, the pair ripping off shots as needed to keep the cultists honest and back behind the cover of the wall.

While Phraim-'Eh's disciples piled up in the halls at their brethren's backs, the corridor between them and the crew had been unceremoniously turned into a killing field. There was no way for them to clear the distance between the corner and the administration section without being gunned down.

"You got that?" Jiya asked Reynolds.

"Sure, I'm not going anywhere," he replied, lazily shooting down the hall anytime a cultist dared to pop his head out. "Take your time."

Jiya chuckled, and she and Maddox angled around the

room, out of the line of fire, and started searching the place.

"Damn, this place is prehistoric," the general muttered as he dug through file cabinets and rifled through papers left on the desks scattered around the room.

"Too damn cold for computers," Jiya joked as she did the same, using her suit's scanners to examine each document quickly before discarding it.

"Waste of resources out here, more likely," Reynolds said from his post at the door. "This here is the sticks. They probably wipe their ass with rolls of brown paper towels, extra rough."

"Which only makes me glad it's so cold out here," Maddox stated. "There's no smelling any of that."

The two continued to search as the cultists piled up down the hall. They looked ready to abandon any sense of tactics and rush forward as a group, hoping that some of them made it close enough to take out the intruders.

It might have been a valid plan if Reynolds and Ka'nak were any less efficient with their hands than they were their weapons.

Which wasn't the case.

"You find anything?" the AI asked, getting tired of imagining the scenarios the cultists might be planning in hopes of stopping the ransacking of their master's paperwork.

"Not a damn thing," Jiya told him, shaking her head. "All this crap is invoices and supply recs and busywork bullshit."

"Well, we had to give it a shot," Reynolds replied, shrugging. "We couldn't know that without coming here."

He opened a channel to the ship.

"Get us out of here, Takal," he called up. "We've got bupkis."

"Is it contagious?" the inventor asked. "Do I need to alert Dr. Reynolds?"

Reynolds shook his head in disappointment. "Just transport us home, Takal."

The AI snapped off a couple more shots before he found himself standing on the bridge, pointing a gun at the wall.

He chuckled and holstered his weapon, seeing Ka'nak do the same, a silly grin on his face as he did.

"We're going to have to time that better when we transport in combat, I think," the AI announced. "Someone's liable to get shot up here without clear signals about when we're poofing."

"Any clue as to where Phraim-'Eh is down there?" XO asked.

"Not a one," Reynolds grunted, turning to Tactical. "I'm thinking those cultists down there are feeling the chill right about now. How about we heat them up?"

"A dozen super-toasty missiles coming right up," Tactical replied.

The viewscreen zoomed in on the compound as the missiles hit, turning it into a blazing fireball.

"'Build a man a fire, and he'll be warm for a day. Set a man on fire, and he'll be warm for the rest of his life.' So sayeth the wizened maestro of merriment, Terry Pratchett," Tactical quoted.

The crew burst out laughing as the outpost burned.

It wasn't until XO's hardened voice cut through their amusement that they stopped.

"You remember how I asked if you'd found anything about Phraim-'Eh's whereabouts a minute ago?" the XO asked.

Reynolds quirked an eyebrow. "Yeah?"

"Well, I think I just found him," XO told him.

"Where?"

"Right outside," XO said.

The viewscreen shifted to show a massive armada of alien ships Gating in around the planet, a massive command ship too similar to the design of the *Pillar* to be coincidence in the lead.

"Oh, fuck me," Reynolds muttered.

CHAPTER FIFTEEN

Thirteen massive ships appeared in the space over Hajh, and there was absolutely no doubt in Reynolds' mind that they belonged to Phraim-'Eh.

"Guess we got his attention," the AI said, staring out at the fleet as it maneuvered to challenge the SD *Reynolds*.

"I'd say so," Jiya commented.

"No time like the present to punch a god in the nose," Tactical said.

Before anyone could stop him, he opened fire on the command ship with everything he had except the ESD.

The ship's shields flared in response, deflecting the vast majority of the SD *Reynolds*' power. The other ships started forward to defend their leader.

"I've fed the tracking rounds into the railguns again," Takal reported over the comm, "seeing as how I don't see us standing our ground here for long." He paused. "Not to be presumptuous, of course."

The SD *Reynolds*' shields were rattled by a wave of incoming fire, shaking the bridge and dimming the lights.

"No, I don't think you're being presumptuous at all, Takal," the AI answered. "You and Xyxl wouldn't have something to show me regarding your long-distance romance, would you?"

"Not yet, I'm afraid," the inventor came back. "Our collaboration is quite enlightening, but the code is proving to be quite daunting, and my Gulg companion and I are struggling with a key piece of it."

"That sucks," Reynolds grunted. "Guess we'll make do with what we have." The android turned to Tactical. "Keep hitting the motherfucker and warm up the ESD. We're going to need some shit-eating death right about now."

The ship rattled again as another wave of fire pounded its shields despite Ria's efforts to evade.

There was little she could do with so many ships closing on them the way they were.

Then the onslaught faded without warning, an unexpected lull settling over the battlefield.

"We're being hailed," Comm announced, explaining the sudden break in combat. "The name of his ship is the *Godhand*, interestingly enough."

"Really? How egotistical," Reynolds said, raising an eyebrow. "I wonder if this prick is looking to monologue?"

"Maybe he'll spill all his plans, and we can kill him while he talks," XO offered.

"Put it onscreen but don't stop moving, Ria. We're not getting shot up while he chats our ears off," Reynolds said.

The crew was silent as Phraim-'Eh appeared on the viewscreen, a gloating smile affixed to his lips. The crew looked upon his visage for the very first time.

He looked a lot like someone from Lariest.

His skin was a deep, bruised red, and he wore his jet-black hair long. It flowed over his shoulders like water. Pits of absolute blackness peered at the crew from over the jagged ridges of his cheekbones.

It wasn't until he opened his mouth and revealed the rows of small, sharpened teeth that he shed the appearance of Jiya's people.

He was clearly something else.

"We meet at long last, Reynolds," Phraim-'Eh said, the power of his voice seeming to lower the temperature on the bridge by a few degrees.

"The pleasure's all yours, I'm sure," Reynolds replied.

Despite everything, he hadn't expected to come face to face with the wannabe god just yet.

He didn't look all that impressive, Reynolds had to admit, but there was a definite aura to the being that spoke of power.

Of course, that might have something to do with the thirteen ships arrayed around the superdreadnought.

Or it could be gas.

Well, if Reynolds weren't an android.

"You have caused me much grief," Phraim-'Eh continued. "It will be my honor to grind your synthetic bones to dust and send your burning ship crashing to the planet below, your crew screaming in its bowels."

"Descriptive," Reynolds said, nodding. "You have a gift for fiction, it appears. Kind of like this fantasy of you taking us out before we get you. Now, *that* is one hell of a story. I don't want to spoil the ending for you, but the one thing I can tell you is that you're the one who's getting his ass kicked."

"You mask your fear with humor. How human of you, android."

Reynolds chuckled. "I'm an artificial intelligence, buddy. I don't know fear, but nice try psychoanalyzing me."

Phraim-'Eh snarled, the first sign of Reynolds getting under his skin.

The AI grinned.

"I was disappointed when Jora'nal failed to destroy you, but now I find myself believing it to be providence that his death has allowed me to do the deed personally," Phraim-'Eh said.

Reynolds' grin turning into full-blown laughter. "Joke's on you, asshole. Your little buddy Jora'nal is still alive. We've got him locked up tight in one of our cells aboard the ship here. He's been singing us a beautiful song about you and all your installations."

Seeing Phraim-'Eh's face darken with rage and surprise thrilled Reynolds, and he thought about recording the image for posperity.

Bethany Anne would get a good laugh out of watching this so-called god shit himself.

The screen went black then, the connection severed.

The weapons fire resumed with a fury.

"I'm thinking you pissed him off by letting him know his puppet was still alive," XO warned.

"Guess he's trying to solve a couple of his problems at once," Reynolds said.

"I'd rather he didn't," Jiya said with a laugh.

"Any luck with the tracer rounds?" Reynolds asked.

"None," Tactical responded. "The ship's shields are too

damn powerful. It's not helping that his destroyers are closing him off, putting themselves between him and us."

"All we need is a crack in his shield," Reynolds stated, examining the data scrolling across the screen in front of him.

"Not sure we'll get the chance, Captain," Maddox warned. "We're getting pounded."

The ship shuddered as if to emphasize the general's point, and the lights flickered.

Reynolds snarled as he examined his options. Without backup or an ace up his sleeve to turn the odds in his favor, he couldn't see standing his ground against Phraim-'Eh's fleet as being a smart choice, no matter how much he wanted to blow that bastard apart.

He wasn't ready to turn tail and run just yet, however.

"Bring us about and prepare the Gate drive, Ensign!" he ordered. "Tactical, have the tracer rounds ready to go."

"What are you thinking, Reynolds?" Jiya asked.

"We need to mix things up. Be creative," the AI replied. "We can't take these guys head-on, but we also can't afford to lose track of them now that we have Phraim-'Eh in our sights, either."

Reynolds took a second to process a million ideas, discounting all but one.

It wasn't without its risks.

"Follow the coordinates I'm feeding you, Ensign, and be ready to Gate again on my command," he told Ria.

"Yes, sir," she replied, always willing to follow an order.

More fire rained down on the SD *Reynolds*, and if it hadn't been for the ensign's slick maneuvering, Reynolds knew they'd be taking far more damage than they were. As it was, there were damage reports streaming in from all over the ship.

There were no casualty reports, though, for which he was grateful.

He didn't want to lose anyone this time around, especially without Xyxl being there to bring them back before they truly died.

"Gate!" Reynolds ordered.

Ria didn't hesitate.

Seconds later, they appeared nearly nose to nose with Phraim-'Eh's command ship, the *Godhand*.

"Holy fuck!" Asya shouted as the ship filled the viewscreen, looming directly ahead of them. "Didn't see that coming."

"I'm hoping Phraim-'Eh didn't either," Reynolds commented, motioning to Tactical. "Hit them with the ESD."

Tactical triggered the weapon. Its power hummed through the ship, then it spilled away from the SD *Reynolds* and ripped across the short distance between the two ships.

The *Godhand* reacted with fervor, going into a steep dive.

The ESD strafed its shields, ripping them away from the top of the craft as if they were peeling the lid off a tin can. A wave of energy rippled through the remaining shields, distorting Reynolds' view of the *Godhand*.

It looked as if it were underwater as it dove, scattering the fleet around it as they desperately avoided colliding with their master's ship.

The ESD streaked past the dodging command ship, but the two ships at its back didn't fare as well.

The first took the brunt of the beam head-on, and there was little more than dust and debris left of the destroyer by the time it sliced through the craft.

The other destroyer, offset just a little so as to avoid the bulk of the beam, still felt enough make them regret their positioning.

The ESD beam scraped the entire starboard side of the ship away from stem to stern. The destroyer listed as the whole right side of the craft was evacuated into space, crew included.

Atmosphere streamed from the destroyer's gaping wound.

There would be no saving that ship.

Ria veered off as soon as the ESD died, following the coordinates Reynolds had fed her console.

Tactical didn't wait for Reynolds to follow up, unloading everything he had into the gaping space the ESD had scorched in the *Godhand*'s shields.

Tracer rounds mixed with railgun fire scored the hull of the massive ship and Tactical whooped as he added a few missiles to the mix, making sure to delay their impact so they didn't take out the tracer rounds that had successfully struck home.

Small explosions pattered the hull of the *Godhand*, but Reynolds noted little damage beyond scorched and pocked armor.

"Gate!" Reynolds called.

Ria jumped on the command, and the SD *Reynolds* moved out of the cluster of Phraim-'Eh's fleet and appeared behind it, swinging around to target the engine of the nearest destroyer.

The ESD having bled the SD *Reynolds* dry, Tactical made do with what he had available.

He released a barrage of weapons fire: railguns, missiles, and cannons without discrimination.

The shields of the trailing destroyer lit up and flared out. The ship's engines were next, going out in a flash of explosions that flared and died within seconds. Smoke billowed from the craft and the destroyer shifted, rolling sideways as its pilot struggled to bring the ship under control.

He failed.

The destroyer began to topple, tumbling end over end until it crashed into another of the destroyers.

It sliced through that ship's shields without effort and slammed into the aft section, both destroyers snapping on impact.

Reynolds smiled as the destroyers broke apart and dropped out of the loose formation of Phraim-'Eh's fleet.

Unfortunately, that was the last substantive blow the SD *Reynolds* would land.

The fleet turned about and hammered the superdreadnought, each blow pounding the gravitic shields. It only took a moment before the damage leaked through and ripped at the armored hull.

"We have an atmosphere leak in the rear compartments," Jiya reported. "Crew is sealing off the section and the bots are working to fix it, but the damage is substantive."

"Shields are fluctuating around fifty percent," Asya

reported. "We can't take another beating like that last round."

"Wounded are reported in the crews' quarters, no deaths," XO called.

"Give it to them one last time, Tactical, then get us the fuck out of here, Ensign," Reynolds ordered, sending escape coordinates to Ria for her to follow. "How's the trace looking, Takal?" he asked over the comm.

"We've got numerous solid connections," the inventor answered after a moment's pause.

"That's going to have to do," the AI answered as Tactical unleashed his full arsenal on the enemy.

It had little effect, the entirety of the fleet advancing and sending back much more fire than the SD *Reynolds* could muster.

"Get us gone!" Reynolds stated.

Ria Gated them out, the SD *Reynolds* shooting across the galaxy before they could take any more damage.

CHAPTER SIXTEEN

The SD *Reynolds* appeared in space over Krokus 4.

"Interesting choice of destinations," Jiya told Reynolds once they caught their breath.

"It's like the greatest hits collection of our journeys," Tactical joked. "What's next, Dal'las Tri?" he asked.

"Ooh, some gambling would be nice," Maddox said wistfully.

The crew turned on him, and he raised his hands in surrender and slumped into his seat.

"I'm kidding. Sheesh. You people can't take a joke."

"The visitations serve two purposes," Reynolds explained as the view of the watery planet filled the screen. "The first is that we have already cleared these locations of overt cult activity. That means our presence will not be immediately reported to Phraim-'Eh, and now that he can't trace us, it gives us a nice place to recuperate. Getting to examine the impact we had upon the system is a secondary but relevant reason for returning. It's always my hope that we have bettered the system by visiting it rather than having harmed it."

"Bringing us into orbit around the planet," Ria announced.

"Belay that," Reynolds told her. "Do we have hull integrity?"

"Lots of damage in the aft section, but we don't have any holes," Jiya reported.

Reynolds nodded. "Then takes us down to the planet, Ensign. I want to put down in the water and drop to the ocean's floor outside of Ocelora."

"That'll make their day, I bet—a superdreadnought parked in their garden," Maddox commented, chuckling.

"Comm, reach out to the Krokan rep, Flor, and let her know we're popping in," Reynolds told his personality.

"No need," Comm responded. "Colonel Raf is reaching out to us. I'm putting him on screen."

"Hello again, Reynolds," Colonel Gar Raf called across the channel from the bridge of his ship, the *Alfar*. "Good to see you. Didn't expect you back so soon."

"Greetings, Colonel," Reynolds shot back. "Didn't expect to be here so soon. We need a place to set down and make repairs. Mind if we hang out a while?"

"I'll contact Flor and have her make arrangements," Raf told him.

"I'd appreciate it," Reynolds replied, then changed tack. "I notice you don't have a defensive barrier up yet. Everything okay with the plans?"

"Oh, absolutely," the colonel answered. "We're just still in the process of fine-tuning the systems. We'll be starting in on construction soon enough. Without the Orau bombing the hell out of us, we've been able to take our time and ensure the system is perfect before putting it in place."

"Roger that," Reynolds shot back. "It's not exactly a simple build."

"No, it's not. Anyway, Flor's signaled she can meet you on the surface and ferry you down to Ocelora from there."

"We, uh, kind of have a different idea, Colonel," Reynolds countered. "Have her meet us on the ocean floor. We'll be the big-ass ship sitting there."

Colonel Raf chuckled, nodding. "I'll forward the message. Take care, Reynolds. I'm sure we'll speak before you leave. Out."

The colonel closed the channel, and Reynolds turned to Ria. "Set us down in the water." He paused for a second, then added, "Carefully."

Ria acknowledged the order with a laugh and began the descent. She broke through the atmosphere of Krokus 4 and dropped until the superdreadnought loomed over the ocean before easing off the throttle.

The SD *Reynolds* slowed and hovered over the ocean's surface for several moments as Ria checked and double-checked the damage reports before she eased into the water.

There was a moment of mild turbulence as the ship adjusted from air to water, and then they were in the depths, drifting down toward the ocean floor.

"Never going to get tired of that view," Jiya remarked, watching the ocean swirl around them as they descended. "Looks even better from inside the ship." She laughed, remembering the first time she and the crew had come to Krokus 4.

It hadn't really been all that long ago.

But like all the other places they'd visited, obvious changes had already taken shape.

Asya zoomed in on Ocelora, the great underwater city of the Krokans. The most noticeable difference was that it didn't look like a bombed-out husk, as it had the last time.

Where there had been char and scorched buildings marring the beauty of the city, new buildings rose up, shiny and clean, at odds with the war-torn appearance it had had so recently.

The superdreadnought settled on the ocean floor as the crew stared out at the city, glad to see it had prospered during their time away.

That was when they noticed that a second, smaller city had been tacked onto the first. It sat near where the crew had slipped out from under the watch of President Jaer Pon's guards and visited Lek's people in the underwater mountain.

In fact, several long tunnel-like appendages reached from the mountain to the new city rising in the ocean.

"I guess everyone's getting along better now that Jaer Pon has been deposed," Maddox commented. "I wonder how Shal Ura and Roe are doing?"

"Think they are still in charge?" Geroux asked.

"It was up to the people to decide but, if you ask me, I'd say they still are," Asya remarked. "Those two were the best candidates."

"Well, a lot can change quickly, as we're noticing," Reynolds warned. "But we'll find out soon enough."

"One of those underwater ferries is approaching," XO reported. "I think you'll have to take a shuttle out if you want to catch a ride, or I can seal off a small section of the hangar bay and pressurize it so they can come inside."

"Scan that bubble first," Reynolds told him.

"Hmm. It's like a forcefield, but not really. It's essentially a reinforced air bubble."

"I thought that might be the case." Reynolds laughed. "Hey, Takal, you think you're ready to transport us to a moving vehicle if you have a clear view of the landing zone?"

"What's the worst that can happen?" Takal answered.

"Death, suffocation, crushed by the pressure of the ocean, eaten by sharks…" Tactical started.

"Rhetorical question, Tactical," Takal told him. "I can certainly try, Reynolds."

"Then plant us in the center of that bubble coming toward us," Reynolds ordered.

"What the hell?" Jiya said. "You only live once, right?"

Fortunately, Takal waited until the crew was armored up and had their helmets on before transporting them across the distance between the ship and the underwater bubble Flor had sent for them. Reynolds, Geroux, Maddox, Ka'nak, and Jiya appeared dead center in it.

However, they were about an inch above the surface.

They gasped and fell the short distance to the floor with loud *thumps*.

"Off by a smidgen," Reynolds reported once they'd touched down.

"No, you appeared exactly where I intended you to

appear," Takal came back smugly. "Would you rather I risk your toes ending up in the flooring?"

"I'll pass on that," Ka'nak muttered. "Thanks for not crippling my toes, Takal."

"You're welcome," the old inventor replied, no hint of sarcasm in his voice.

The crew rode the bubble all the way to Ocelora, where it slipped inside one of the many docks set next to the city and docked.

As the water drained away, Reynolds spied Lek standing alongside Flor on the other side of the barrier that kept the ocean from spilling into Ocelora. They greeted them once the dock had drained and the crew stepped into the city proper.

Lek gave them all a powerful hug, moving through the crew one by one, and Flor smiled at them, prim and proper.

"Good to see you all," Flor told them. "President Roe and Vice President Shal Ura are looking forward to seeing you again."

"That answers *that* question, then," Geroux said with a smile. "I love a happy ending."

Flor and Lek led them through the city, showing it off as they did. The tour confirmed what the crew had seen from the bridge of the SD *Reynolds*.

The vast majority of the damage caused by the Orau bombardments had been fixed and cleaned up, making the city appear as though it were new.

Gone were the bombed-out sections of town, and in their place stood bright new homes and businesses that made the beautiful city even more appealing.

There was no mistaking that the Krokans had made the most of their time out from under the cruel thumb of the Orau and their shithead leader, Jaer Pon.

Reynolds was glad to see how things had progressed.

He'd been proud of their efforts, and while his mind was focused on Phraim-'Eh and how they would defeat the bastard, getting to see the successes were exhilarating.

It brought a clarity of purpose to his mission he believed Bethany Anne would appreciate.

They were leaving the universe a better place than when they'd found it.

He couldn't hope for a better legacy.

Well, that wasn't entirely true.

Leaving the universe a better place *and* blowing the fuck out of Phraim-'Eh and his minions would be a better legacy.

They arrived at the presidential palace a short while later, and Reynolds was glad to see that it looked the exact same as it had before.

The new rulers hadn't spent a dime on the grand palace. Rather, they had focused all their effort on making the homes of the people better before turning their eyes inward.

Reynolds was proud of the young couple.

The crew was led inside, and Jiya thrilled to see the statues were still in place. They'd been shined a bit, cleaned up and dusted, and that only added to the impression they made, stoic and poised as the crew strode past.

This time around, the statues better resembled the actual people of Krokus 4, the war-weary countenances of the populace now more closely matching the prouder, stronger visages of the statues that lined corridors of the presidential compound.

Jiya ran her hand over the statues as they passed.

They were led into the throne room, and the first thing Reynolds noticed was that the dais had been removed, putting the leaders on the level of the populace they'd be meeting with.

Flor led them up the carpeted aisle to the far end of the room, where Shal Ura and Roe stood before their seats, awaiting the crew.

"Greetings!" Shal Ura called as they arrived, gesturing for the crew to sit down in the chairs that splayed out in front of the presidential seats.

Roe smiled at them, letting them take their seats before speaking.

Servants came over and offered drinks.

"I like what you've done with the place," Reynolds told the pair, gesturing toward the missing dais.

"Seemed appropriate," Shal Ura replied. "Especially after all we've been through."

Lek chuckled behind them.

"How have you been?" Roe asked, meeting the eyes of each of the crew in turn.

The group chatted informally for several minutes, catching up on the time between visits until they'd exhausted all the small talk.

When a lull in the conversation appeared, Shal Ura turned to Reynolds. "I presume you saw the additions outside the city?"

"I did, indeed," the AI replied. "Looks to me like you've tied your two societies together."

"That's precisely what we've done," Shal Ura stated. "Now that the Orau threat is gone, we decided it would be best to reconcile with our brothers and sisters and connect our worlds, as they always should have been."

"Seems you succeeded, if the grin on Lek's face is any indication," Jiya teased.

"It's nice not having to sneak into Ocelora to visit family," Lek told them. "Now I simply ride the tube over, and no one tries to shoot me. Well, no one but my ex-wife." She laughed.

Reynolds grinned. "And how about the people on Krokus 1? How are they progressing?"

"We're in regular contact with them, and they're doing well. They're prospering, at their own pace," Roe explained with a grin. "Colonel Raf and his people helped them get situated and built them a better outpost to live in, and we send regular supplies to them to keep them healthy and fed. Beyond that, they are building their own lives out there, happy and content and free from the damaging influences of the Orau invaders."

"That's good to hear," Reynolds replied.

"Speaking of damaging influences," Shal Ura started, "Colonel Raf noted the condition of your craft. Is there anything we can do to help with repairs?"

"Appreciate that, but we mostly need a place to lay low while we repair it and make plans," Reynolds explained. "We've stirred up some shit, and we need a few days to figure out our next move."

"Then you have it," Roe assured them. "You're welcome here for as long as you want to stay."

"And if you need anything else, don't hesitate to ask, Reynolds," Shal Ura told the AI. "We're in your debt."

Reynolds shook his head. "Not at all, but we are grateful for the kindness. We'll stay out of the way while we fix our ship and scheme," the AI said with a laugh. "You won't even know we're here."

"Absolutely unnecessary," Roe replied. "We're happy to have you, and we can entertain your crew while you work to repair your ship. We have plenty of room to transfer over as many of them as you want while you're here."

"That's very generous of you," the AI told her. "We'll likely take you up on the offer. Most of the crew rarely get a chance to leave the ship since our stops are usually fairly short. They'd be delighted."

"Then consider it done," Shal Ura confirmed.

Reynolds nodded his thanks.

"It's probably best we be off to get to work, but we'll coordinate the transportation of our crew to the city at your convenience," the AI told the pair. "And if *you* need anything, please, let us know. We're happy to provide anything we can in return for your kindness."

The presidents thanked them, and Reynolds and the crew returned to the *Reynolds* to prepare for their next encounter.

There was simply too much to do for the primary crew to lounge around now that they had Phraim-'Eh in their sights.

That evening, once all the arrangements between the ship and the Krokans had been finalized, Reynolds summoned his crew to a meeting room to discuss their plans.

Jiya strolled in first, along with Geroux and Asya. Takal joined them a short while later, setting a small computer down on the table in front of him. Ka'nak and Maddox dragged in last and plopped into seats.

Reynolds stood at the head of the table, looking at the crew as they settled in. Cups of Jiya's favorite coffee littered the table.

The AI figured they might need the caffeine.

"Now that we've finally gotten the chance to sit down and discuss things, what do you think of our enemy?" Reynolds asked.

"Speaking for myself, he doesn't look like any god I've ever imagined," Jiya admitted. "Of course, him flying in with a fleet of thirteen ships didn't exactly instill awe, either. What kind of god needs that many warships to make himself feel good?"

"He's overcompensating for something if you ask me." Asya chuckled.

"A small godhood?" Ka'nak asked, laughing.

"Kind of what I was thinking," Reynolds told them. "He's hiding behind a hell of a lot of firepower for a guy passing himself off as a deity."

"That doesn't make him any less dangerous, though," Maddox said. "Thirteen are a lot of ships."

"Only nine now," Jiya corrected, "but I realize that doesn't change much. It's still a lot of ships to face off against."

"Ships we can now track, and which remain in orbit

around Hajh," Takal grinned. "I've examined the tracer rounds, and while many of them were cleaned off or deactivated by the automatic repair systems of the *Godhand*, over thirty are still active."

Takal opened his computer and turned it around so everyone could see it.

"I took a moment to better adapt the tracer rounds after our first failure at using them when I realized I could do more than simply trace them," he said. "I implanted small scanners, which emit pulses too low and infrequent to be detected."

"To what end?" Reynolds asked.

"They will give us snippets of intelligence regarding the fleet above and beyond their location," Takal explained. "Because they are pulsed to avoid being found, the updates will not be in real time or even consistent, but it might provide us with information regarding their efforts and actions while we prepare to face them again.

"And since we used Gulg technology to craft them, they will continue to transmit their locations, no matter where in the universe the *Godhand* travels."

"Speaking of the Gulg," Reynolds interrupted. "Has Xyxl approached his people with our request yet?"

"He has, and they have agreed," Takal answered.

"Excellent." Reynolds rubbed his hands together diabolically. "And the coding?"

"We've had a breakthrough, but it's premature to say the process is complete," the inventor went on. "Geroux and I will work on it more while we await Xyxl, but I believe it will only be a matter of weeks before it is fully functional."

"We don't have weeks," Reynolds reminded him. "I need you to push harder and get the program done, Takal."

"I'll do what I can." The inventor climbed out of his seat. "Speaking of which, I should get back to it."

Reynolds nodded, and Takal left to return to his work.

"So, what's our next move, boss?" Jiya asked. "We going to wait here until we're ready to take Phraim-'Eh on again?"

The AI shook his head. "We won't be prepared to face down all of Phraim-'Eh's ships until Xyxl and Takal come through."

"Then we're staying put?" Asya asked.

"Nope," Reynolds told her. "We've got Phraim-'Eh's people scrambling, and part of the mission is to eradicate *all* of the Kurtherian influence he's introduced to the universe. I think we keep the old god on his toes and hit the next target in line. As long as we know where Phraim-'Eh's ships are, we can lash out at his holdings with impunity."

The crew agreed.

"Once the ship is fully repaired, we'll head out," Reynolds said. "Who's up for a game of Whack-A-Cultist?"

CHAPTER SEVENTEEN

The repairs were finalized two days later, and Reynolds and the crew said their goodbyes to the Krokans, promising to return soon.

Once that was done, they set off again, returning to space and Gating through to the final cult installation on their list, Suri.

Alarms sounded as soon as they entered open space above the planet.

"No sneaking up on folks here," Asya said. "They clocked us the second we exited the Gate, Captain. We've got four destroyers headed our way already, weapons armed."

"No hails," Comm reported.

"How rude," Reynolds replied, shaking his head. "The least they can do is say hi before they try to fuck us. Dinner would be nice, too."

"They're serving up a meal of hot lead, from the looks of it," Tactical said. "Although I have to question why they're firing already when they aren't in range yet."

Reynolds looked at the screen and confirmed what his other personality was saying. The enemy ships had already engaged the SD *Reynolds*, despite not being close enough to have any accuracy or do any damage.

What few shots did reach the ship were easily deflected by the gravitic shields, the blows not even testing their integrity.

"Maybe Phraim-'Eh's got them all riled up," Jiya suggested. "The shithead might not be that scary to us, but he sure seems to whip his converts into a frenzy everywhere we go."

Reynolds nodded absently, but he wasn't sure that was the case here. Something was off, but he couldn't put his finger on it.

"Scan the planet," he ordered. "Let me know what's going on down there."

"These seem to be the only ships they have that are big enough to threaten us," Jiya replied after a short pause. "There's a large installation down there, a lot of people and equipment, but it's not geared up like Rolant was. I'm only pinpointing a tiny fraction of the AA installations we faced down there."

"And none of them are even trying to target us, if my readings are correct," Maddox added.

"You think we have them spooked?" Asya asked. "We have been hitting these guys hard for months now, and even more so lately."

Reynolds shrugged, but he felt there was something to Asya's theory.

"Let's find out," he suggested. "I want to Gate in and hit them from the flank. Let's test their mettle."

"Setting coordinates," Ria replied. "Done," she added a moment later.

"Do it," Reynolds commanded.

The SD *Reynolds* Gated and appeared off the starboard side of the rearmost destroyer. Ria brought the super-dreadnought right up on top of the enemy ship, and Tactical let loose.

He pounded the ship with railgun fire to soften its shields and followed up with missiles.

Caught off-guard, the destroyer veered off the wrong way, leaving it in the line of fire longer than it would have been had it turned the opposite direction. It left its weak-shield side vulnerable for far too long without reinforcing it.

Reynolds saw panic in the motion, and the destroyer paid for it with every life aboard.

Explosions tore up the side of the enemy ship, cracking its hull and blasting pieces of its armored shell into space. Its guts hemorrhaged and spewed its air into space in giant, frothing vents.

The ship broke along the lines where Tactical had struck it, and the two halves of the destroyer tumbled away, out of control, forever to be entombed in the cold of space.

The rest of the ships swung wide, making an effort to turn about and face the SD *Reynolds*, but it was a lazy effort and half-assed. They weren't in any mood to rush now that they had seen their companion ship blown away.

"I guess there's a limit to people's fanaticism," Jiya commented.

"Staring down the barrel of the loaded gun of their

leader all the time is stressful," Maddox said. "After a while, I can imagine folks just want an end to it. Sometimes that manifests in them charging in and taking their chances. Other times, they realize the futility of it all and put their hands up and surrender or simply run away."

"Let's find out which type of people these are," Reynolds ordered. "Hail the lead ship, Comm. Let's see if they'll reply."

Several long moments passed, Reynolds believing the enemy would rather face their fate than talk, and then Comm's voice rang out.

"I've got the commander of the *Stark* on the line," Comm announced.

"Put him through," Reynolds said.

An older soldier appeared on the screen. His hair was trimmed perfectly, and the slim mustache on his upper lip was manicured into what was almost a perfectly straight line.

Reynolds noted the shine of his regalia and the crispness of his uniform as he appraised the soldier, but his face didn't match the spotless image he portrayed.

He looked tired and worn, and it wasn't until he spoke that Reynolds realized the captain really wasn't all that old. He was simply beaten down and exhausted.

"I am Captain Frair Rom of the *Stark*," he said. His voice was neutral, but there was no vigor to it. "You have intruded upon his Eternal Majesty Phraim-'Eh's territory. You are advised to turn about immediately, or we will be forced to destroy you."

"How'd that work out for the fourth member of your

fleet?" Reynolds fired back, meeting the captain's gaze and holding it. "We can send you to join him if you like."

The captain swallowed visibly and ran a nervous hand across his clean-shaved chin. "You cannot frighten us, Captain Reynolds," Rom assured the AI, but Reynolds didn't believe a fucking word the guy said.

"If that's the case, why haven't you and your ships come at us again?" he challenged. "You clearly know who we are, since I didn't introduce myself but you said my name. That being the case, you know damn well your master wants us dead, so why are you offering us an out?"

"Phraim-'Eh's fleet is still parked above Hajh," Tactical reported in his ear. "If this guy is hoping for the cavalry to swoop in and rescue him, he's shit outta luck."

Reynolds acknowledged Tactical with the barest of nods.

"This is your last opportunity," Rom warned, straightening and doing his best to glare menacingly into the camera.

"How about I counter your generous offer with one of my own?" the AI asked. "We both know damn well your master is camped out at Hajh, and he's not coming to save your asses. By the time he gets here, there will be nothing left of you or your outpost except crispy bits and ashes."

Reynolds let the threat sink in for a moment before continuing.

"*Or*...you can surrender and live," Reynolds finished, the offer simple and to the point.

The captain continued to stare at Reynolds as if incapable of speaking.

"Guess we're doing this the hard way, then."

Reynolds motioned to Ria. "Ensign Alcott, bring us about so we can blow these fools away up close and personal."

"Yes, sir!" Ria cried.

Jiya stifled a grin at the young ensign's excitement. A message scrolled across her station, advising her to ignore the order but to act as if she were complying.

"Targeting the lead ship," Tactical announced, doing exactly that, knowing the captain would know otherwise.

There was little more than a heartbeat of silence before the *Stark*'s captain broke it.

"Forgive me, Lord," he whispered barely loud enough for anyone to hear, eyes downcast. Then he braved a look up and met Reynolds' gaze again. "I surrender," he said. "*We* surrender," he corrected.

The captain turned to an officer Reynolds couldn't see offscreen.

"Advise the fleet to stand down," Captain Rom said before turning back to Reynolds.

Fleet?

The AI wiped away his grin before the captain saw it.

I'd hardly call three ships a fleet, but I'll let the guy have his moment of vanity. What can it hurt?

"Weapons are going offline," Asya reported. "As are their shields."

"This feel a little too easy to anyone else?" Tactical asked, muting the channel so Captain Rom couldn't hear him.

"It does seem a little abrupt," XO admitted.

"Then again," Jiya added, "we *have* been leaving all sorts of cultists' bodies in our wake."

Reynolds unmuted the channel and stared at the captain. "If you're serious about surrendering, here are our terms."

The AI gave the captain a moment to balk, but instead, he only nodded.

"You will abandon your ships and return to the planet, leaving them behind to be destroyed."

Reynolds paused again, and although the captain was visibly shaken by what he'd been told, he didn't contest it.

"You will then denounce your god and abandon his faith, vowing to never again take up arms for him."

One last hesitation told Reynolds the captain was serious when all he got was a quiet, almost whimpering cough as the terms were laid out.

"Abide by those terms, and you will live out your life in peace from here on out," Reynolds closed. "Since we intend to kill Phraim-'Eh and anyone who maintains their allegiance to him, your choice is clear. Step away or die."

It wasn't much of a choice, but the captain made the right one.

"We will abide by your terms, Captain Reynolds," Rom told him, his chin angling toward his chest in shame.

The channel went black, and Reynolds turned to face the crew, an eyebrow raised.

"Maybe I'm just a pessimist, but that was definitely too damn easy, just like Tactical and XO said," Maddox stated. "He gave in without any kind of fight at all."

"Maybe they're tired of fighting?" Jiya suggested.

"I'm with Maddox on this one," Asya countered.

"You think he really means it?" Ria asked Reynolds.

The AI shrugged. "Honestly? It doesn't really matter,"

he replied as the first of the shuttles emerged from the enemy destroyers, angling toward the planet. "Either we take out Phraim-'Eh and these cultists have no one to follow anymore, or Phraim-'Eh stops by and murders them all for being cowardly betrayers. Either suits our purpose."

More and more shuttles emerged from the destroyers, and Reynolds watched the reports as Jiya scanned the ships for lifeforms. With the shields down, it was a simple task.

"Any signs of self-destructs being triggered or people trying to stay aboard?" Reynolds asked.

"Negative," Jiya responded. "It appears they are doing exactly what they agreed to. Well, the first part, at least. No real way to know about the second."

Reynolds nodded, also surprised at how easy it had been to take the planet without having to fire more than enough shots to destroy a single ship.

"Scrape the command ship's databases, but be sure to scan the uploads to make sure there's nothing harmful in the coding," Reynolds told Geroux. "My inner paranoid is telling me to be careful, while my inner optimist doesn't give a fuck as long as shit works out in our favor."

"That could be what they want us to do," Asya suggested. "I mean, they had to know we'd plunder their systems before we destroyed the ships. That's just standard practice, right?"

"Well, we already know enough about their coding to recognize and defend against it, so it's not like uploading a virus is much of a game-changer," Reynolds replied with a shrug. "Besides, if that's their big, nefarious scheme, we're seriously overestimating Phraim-'Eh."

"Databases copied and decrypted," Geroux reported. "I'm parsing the information now."

"Blow those ships away, Tactical," Reynolds ordered. "No point letting them sit there while we pick our asses."

Tactical complied and fired on each ship in turn. With no shields up, they were sitting ducks.

It took a moment for him to batter past the armor, but it wasn't long before all three ships were rattling hunks of junk, tumbling toward a fiery death in the atmosphere of Suri.

"That was fun." Tactical chuckled.

"I think I've got something, Captain," Geroux said.

She brought it up on the screen.

"A location in the *Stark*'s data coincides with one of the smaller cult installation's coordinates we scraped from Jora'nal's computer."

"What are we looking at?" the AI asked.

"It's some tiny, out-of-the-way planet that's barely a blip on the star charts," Geroux explained. "A planet that doesn't even register as having a real name, only a designation. QI482, but the corresponding logs reference it as 'Quil.'"

Reynolds looked it up.

"An agricultural planet?" he asked, reading the information scrolling across the screen. "No exports, nothing of note has ever been recorded regarding it, and it's *way* outside the space lanes. There is *literally* nothing there."

"Sounds like a perfect home base for a cult, if you ask me," Asya said.

"It's a trap!" Tactical shouted.

"It's no fun when they don't get the reference, Tactical."

"Not my fault they were born in the wrong galaxy…far, far away."

Reynolds groaned. "Just stop, please."

"We could always go and check it out," Jiya suggested. "We've still got the trackers on Phraim-'Eh, and we'll know if he responds to our invading his space. If he doesn't, then we blow up the outpost there, and we're another batch of dead cultists ahead with no loss to us."

Reynolds stiffened, suddenly grinning. "That gives me an idea."

"That's never good," Tactical muttered.

CHAPTER EIGHTEEN

Phraim-'Eh sat in his quarters aboard the *Godhand*.

Still stationed over Hajh, he had his disciples scouring through the wreckage Reynolds and his people had made of the outpost below. And though there was little left to parse through, Phraim-'Eh had to be absolutely certain that the Federation scum received no additional intelligence from the out-of-the-way station.

He'd once believed his whereabouts to be sacrosanct to his top disciples, that they would never betray him to the Federation or his other enemies, but that illusion had been shattered by Jora'nal.

It had been further stomped upon by the revelation that Jora'nal still lived and was in the AI's custody.

He wanted to think the Federation pawn had lied to him, that he'd only been baiting him when he said that, but evidence from the site of Jora'nal's failure spoke of Reynolds' escape from the planet right before the explosion that wiped out the headquarters there.

That meant that, if Reynolds could have slipped free,

then so could Jora'nal, especially if the AI took the disciple with him.

He wondered if the fool was working for Reynolds, being fed promises and lies to cooperate, or if the foul creature had suffered and broken under torture.

Does it matter? he asked himself.

That Jora'nal would betray him in either event was sufficient to consider him lost.

And if he were still alive when Phraim-'Eh was finished dealing with Reynolds and his crew, Phraim-'Eh would see to it that Jora'nal met a fate fit for scum like him.

A smile crept to Phraim-'Eh's lips as he imagined what he might do to Jora'nal, but a quiet knock at the door tore him from his pleasant reverie.

"Come!" he shouted.

A servant eased the door open just wide enough to peek inside.

"The Voice wishes to speak with you," the male said.

"Patch him through," Phraim-'Eh replied, waving the servant away. He was all too glad to comply.

Phraim-'Eh opened the channel without waiting for the servant. Quiet static became an even quieter voice after a moment.

"Speak, Voice," Phraim-'Eh commanded, too sick with disappointment to be bothered to threaten him.

It clearly did no good, and the Voice would feel Phraim-'Eh's wrath soon enough. Until then, he served a purpose.

"Reynolds has been to Suri," the Voice reported.

"And?" Phraim-'Eh nudged when the Voice paused to catch his breath.

"The ships there have been destroyed, and he coerced the captain and his crews to stand down and turn their back on you, Lord."

A growl welled up from deep in Phraim-'Eh's throat. "He did *what?*"

"Captain Rom has turned against you, if only in a promise to Reynolds," the Voice went on.

"Then he has turned against me indeed," Phraim-'Eh swore. "I will see the captain and all his people dead! Prepare to meet me, for I am coming to Suri now!"

"If I might..." the Voice pleaded.

"You dare?"

"Only so that you might not be blinded by your rage before you know everything I have learned, Master," the Voice told him.

Phraim-'Eh nearly choked on his fury, but he reined it in enough to allow his disciple to speak and explain himself.

"Tell me!"

"Reynolds has learned of Quil, Master," his disciple told him. "Captain Rom overheard him saying as they banished him to Suri that their next target would be Quil. The captain prays to beg your forgiveness for providing this information."

A cold chill froze the blood in Phraim-'Eh's veins. "How...could..." He left his question hanging, all thoughts of the captain's betrayal vanquished from his mind.

His stomach churned as he imagined Reynolds defiling his home planet, ruining the system as the android's masters had ruined countless others by bringing their warped sense of justice to them.

"This cannot be allowed," Phraim-'Eh said, more to himself than the Voice. He barely remembered the disciple was on the line. "He cannot be allowed to defile the home of my forefathers. They struggled long and hard to find a world where they could hide from the clawing fingers of the Federation, where they could feel safe at long last. I will not let them soil Quil! I will *not*!"

Phraim-'Eh leapt to his feet, his power barely restrained. He paced back and forth, every step pounding across the deck and reverberating through the steel.

"Summon every disciple to me," Phraim-'Eh ordered, "and call them to war. This *creature* shall not set his blasphemous foot upon my homeworld. I will see him burned to ashes before I let him take my world from me."

"As you wish, Master," the Voice replied, and was forgotten.

Phraim-'Eh screamed for his servant. He would journey to Quil and set an armada about the planet, ensuring Reynolds could never come near.

And for daring to threaten his home, Phraim-'Eh would see the AI burn.

Then he'd turn his fury on the Earth!

CHAPTER NINETEEN

"What do you know?" Reynolds said, pulling a face. "This place really *is* the pathetic god's base of operations."

He tapped the screen that was monitoring Phraim-'Eh's fleet, calling it to the attention of the crew.

"He's pulling up stakes and headed this way like a bat outta Hell," the AI went on. "He didn't even bother to collect the people he'd dropped off on the planet before he took off. Poor bastards."

Ka'nak shrugged. "That's a few less cultists we have to worry about killing, but I'm torn as to whether that's good or bad."

"The trackers show that he is on his way here with all haste," Takal warned.

"Then I guess it's a good thing we showed up before we *convinced* Captain Rom to send that message, huh?" Reynolds laughed.

The SD *Reynolds* had Gated in earlier in the day and laid traps for Phraim-'Eh's fleet. They'd seeded the space around the planet with cloaked mines in the hundreds, and they'd arranged a few other surprises for the would-be god once he arrived.

Phraim-'Eh's panicked reaction to Quil being threatened made it clear that Reynolds had made the right decision.

Since the start of the mission, the cultists and their leader had been the ones to choose the times and places of the engagements between them, and Reynolds and his people had suffered for it.

Good people had died or been injured because Phraim-'Eh had held all the cards, sneaking around the shadows and bleeding his misery into their lives.

Fuck that!

Reynolds had not just slipped an ace up his sleeve, he'd thrown the whole fucking deck out and changed the game.

Now, instead of running and reacting, trying to figure out what was going on, Reynolds had taken control. He'd lured Phraim-'Eh to them.

The planet being the wannabe god's homeworld only made the turnaround that much more satisfying.

The pleasant pastoral planet that hung below was an odd backdrop to such a poignant moment, but Reynolds would take what he could get if it meant getting a real shot at taking out Phraim-'Eh for good.

And he would.

It didn't matter what it took, Reynolds would see this Kurtherian line of evil aborted before it could cause any more harm to the universe than it already had.

It all ended today.

"Where are we, Takal?" he asked over the comm.

"Putting the finishing touches on the program," the

inventor replied. "I only wish I had time to test it. I can't be certain—"

"There aren't any wish-granting genies out here for you to winkle a wish out of, so you're going to have to make sure it works in the sandbox, or we're fucked," Reynolds told him. "We're not going to get more than one shot at this. If it fucks up, we're dead."

"I feel better about it now, thank you," Takal replied snidely.

"Hey, it's what I'm here for," Reynolds shot back. "Seriously, though, this needs to work."

Tactical chuckled. "No pressure."

"Trackers show Phraim-'Eh is nearing the system," Geroux reported.

"I need to get back to the program, then," Takal muttered. "I guess we'll know if it works soon enough," he added before cutting the channel.

"If I were a betting person..." Maddox began.

"Maybe you and Takal can go get a beer," Reynolds told him. "I think at this point, I'd prefer a drunk Takal over a sober one."

"It's not like the fate of our existence lies in his hands or anything," Tactical said. "Right? *Right?*"

"I'm seriously regretting having split my psyche," Reynolds told Tactical. "Well, parts of it, at least."

"Now, now, girls," XO chided. "You're both pretty."

"We've got approximately five minutes before Phraim-'Eh pops in," Geroux called.

"Everything's in place," Asya noted. "There's really nothing we can do but wait."

"That's the worst part of it all," Maddox said. "Put me in

the fight, and I'm fine. Tell me to wait, and the anticipation just sucks the life out of me."

"He'll be here before you know it," Jiya warned, "so stay frosty. We're ready for this."

And they were, Reynolds realized.

Every variable he could control had been rigged their way. Now the only real concerns were luck and the overwhelming power of Phraim-'Eh's armada.

Either could sway the odds away from the SD *Reynolds*, but the AI wouldn't let himself think that way.

He and the crew had survived against all odds since they'd started this mission, and Reynolds would be damned if he failed now.

Not with so much riding on him.

He'd stand over a fallen Phraim-'Eh and deliver the final blow of the battle no matter what.

"Button up, folks," Asya called. "We've got incoming."

Reynolds didn't bother to sound any alarms or dim the lights as they counted down the last few seconds before Phraim-'Eh arrived and engaged them. It wouldn't do anything but heap stress on the crew, and he didn't want to do that to them.

In fact, he contemplated dancing a jig and singing Gaelic battle songs to motivate them, but then he remembered he was a terrible dancer and Takal hadn't designed him with a pleasant singing voice.

Guess I'll just have to lead them to victory, then, he thought with a laugh.

"He's here!" Asya announced.

Phraim-'Eh's command ship Gated in, the rest of his fleet following behind.

That was when the fun started.

Explosions erupted as soon as they arrived, the fleet Gating in close to the planet in order to barricade it against Reynolds' aggression.

They'd walked right into the trap, Phraim-'Eh's impatience getting the best of him.

The cloaked mines wreaked havoc among the enemy ships, forcing them to veer off and break ranks as more and more of the mines went off.

That only pushed the ships into more of them.

A damaged ship filled Reynolds's viewscreen as one of the destroyers ran into the cloaked stash of pucks Reynolds had cobbled together to provide an extra surprise.

It worked perfectly.

The impact tore through the ship's shields and the pucks drilled into the armored hull so effectively that a gaping, venting hole was left behind.

Tactical took the opportunity to fire a salvo of missiles to finish the job the pucks had started.

The destroyer was struck dead on, its flank shredded by the rattling explosions. Listing, the ship veered into more of the mines, which put it out of its misery.

The ship, engines flaring, slowly tumbled away, lifeless.

"Down to nine!" Geroux reported.

It was still too damn many.

Then another of the destroyers was bleeding its atmosphere behind it.

"Using cloaked Pods really ought to be illegal," Tactical said, laughing as Jiya remotely piloted another of the rigged Pods into the side of the destroyer she'd already hit.

"Use what you got, my mama used to say," Reynolds remarked.

"You don't have a mother," Tactical fired back.

"Now you're just being mean. Focus that shit on the bad guys," the AI told him.

"We're taking fire!" Asya announced.

"That asshole, Phraim-'Eh, is one single-minded motherfucker," Jiya noted. "I've got a cure for that."

Jiya maneuvered several of the cloaked Pods through a narrow passageway in the field of mines and set them on a collision course for the *Godhand*.

One was accidentally set off, caught in the crossfire, but the other two slammed into the *Godhand*'s shields and detonated.

The shields absorbed the impact and Phraim-'Eh's ship kept coming, bearing down on the SD *Reynolds*.

"Lure him back into the mine lane," Reynolds told Ria. "Let him think we're retreating."

"On it!" she replied, easing back to draw the *Godhand* in.

The ship shuddered and bucked unexpectedly, and Reynolds was forced to grab the arms of his seat to keep from toppling out.

"What the hell was that?" he called.

"One of the fucking destroyers broke through the minefield and rammed us," Asya explained, rapidly scrolling through the damage reports as Ria compensated for the impact.

Tactical hammered the destroyer for daring to kamikaze them, and Jiya added insult to injury by slamming several of the cloaked Pods into the bridge of the ship.

"Take that!" she shouted as the Pods exploded on the heels of Tactical's missiles.

The destroyer veered off and lost control, drifting through the minefield to end its days in a flash of light.

"Sitrep!" Reynolds demanded.

"The starboard engine is damaged," Asya called. "Down to seventy-eight percent thrust." She growled as she examined the reports streaming in on her screen. "Son of a bitch! That last blow smashed a hole in the aggro center. We lost a couple of printers and about a year's worth of food."

"Please tell me it wasn't the coffee!" Jiya asked, wide-eyed.

"No," Asya replied after a moment. "Looks like it was mostly vegetables."

"No loss there," Ka'nak remarked.

"Hello, scurvy!" Tactical joked. "Welcome aboard."

"The *Godhand*'s still coming," Ria announced.

A ship-rattling blow backed up her statement.

"Shields are buckling on the starboard side," Asya advised. "I'm buffering them with the Gulg techniques, but I'm not sure how long they'll hold."

"They're eating mines, and I've rammed a couple Pods up their ass," Jiya called. "That ship is a beast."

"We might have to pull out the ESD again," Tactical warned.

"It's too soon," Reynolds told him. "Not yet. Hold it in reserve."

"Not much use if we're dead," Tactical said.

Ria veered off as the *Godhand* closed, expertly piloting the superdreadnought through the open spaces between the fields of mines they'd positioned, gaining some distance between the *Godhand* and the *Reynolds*.

"Nice move, Ria!" Asya congratulated. "That's bought us a couple of seconds."

"I'm punching the clock on a few more," Tactical announced as he blasted a wounded destroyer and took it out, sending it careening toward the planet below.

"I hope that fucking thing lands on and kills Phraim-'Eh's favorite cow," XO cursed.

"We're running out of mines," Geroux reported. "They've done a lot of damage, but the enemy is throwing tracers now and clearing them out."

"I'm almost out of rigged Pods, too," Jiya warned as she slammed another of them into a listing destroyer.

That was the final blow against that ship, and it exploded, its damaged hull unable to take any more.

"Seven," Asya called.

"Six and a half, technically," Reynolds corrected. "We've got one drifting who's moved out of firing range. Unless they fix what's wrong soon, they'll be completely out of the fight."

"That's still steep odds," XO noted.

The *Godhand* swept back around then, pounding the SD *Reynolds* with railgun fire from above.

The lights dimmed and alarms sounded. but this time Reynolds didn't bother to address it. He let both go as Ria fought to evade the cult's command ship.

"Anything, Takal?" Reynolds asked over the comm.

"Another minute," he shot back. "Hit a snag. The process is locking up."

"Phraim-'Eh is going to hit us with a snag if you don't hurry up," Reynolds growled.

Ria maneuvered the superdreadnought around, taking advantage of the remaining minefields and managed to get them behind the *Godhand*.

Tactical and Jiya jumped on the opportunity and unleashed everything they had.

Explosions rippled along the rear of the ship, tearing through the shields and scoring the hull. Other than a moral victory, it did little to slow the massive ship down.

"I wished we'd have thought to put explosives on those damn tracer rounds we dotted the *Godhand* with earlier," Tactical said.

"If the missiles and rigged shuttles we're hitting it with aren't taking it down, the tiny bits of explosive we could have added sure as hell wouldn't have done anything." Reynolds shrugged.

"Can we do anything else with those things, Takal?" Jiya asked over the comm.

"Busy here," came the reply, followed by a curt, "No."

"ESD time?" Tactical asked.

"Not yet," Reynolds told him again.

Tactical didn't even bother to complain. He unloaded a salvo of missiles into the rear of the *Godhand* as the flagship evaded, muting most of the damage.

"All the Pods are done!" Jiya advised. "I'm chucking pucks out of the bays to see if we get lucky."

Explosions erupted all around the ship as the remaining mines went up, doing what damage they could.

It was minimal.

The enemy fleet was reforming on their command ship,

and the entire group was coming about, angling attack vectors toward the *Reynolds*.

"I'm going to have to start throwing rocks soon," Tactical called. "Munitions are starting to tank."

"Shields are at forty percent," Asya informed. "Thirty-nine," she corrected as another blast rattled the ship's port side.

"Deaths?" Reynolds asked, even though he didn't want to.

"Negative," Jiya's answer came back. "Our moving all non-essential personnel to the inner quarters and replacing almost every job on the ship with bots has kept our people safe. We've got some injuries, and a few serious ones, unfortunately, but no one has died."

"A damn miracle is what that is," Maddox said.

"We could use another of those right about now," Ka'nak exclaimed.

"Though I don't dare consider my people or me a miracle, I would imagine something like this is what you mean."

Jiya snapped around at the unexpected voice to see Xyxl right after he materialized on the bridge, the *Reynolds'* shields now attuned to allow him to board without resistance no matter their setting.

"You have impeccable timing," Reynolds told the alien. "Now help us take these pieces of shit out!"

"As you wish," Xyxl replied.

Gulg warships appeared in the space above the *Reynolds* then, Gating in and engaging the cult's fleet.

"About damn time!" Ka'nak whooped.

CHAPTER TWENTY

"Three fucking ships?" Reynolds snarled a few seconds later when he realized the entirety of the backup Xyxl had brought with him. "You only brought three ships?"

Xyxl, having shifted his energies into the humanoid Reynolds and the crew were used to, did his best imitation of a shrug.

"I have apparently reached my allotment of starships," the alien explained. "Three was all my people were willing to provide."

"It'll have to do," Reynolds said.

"If it helps, I transported down to Takal's laboratory for a moment before I came here," Xyxl offered. "I aided him with the last of the program we concocted. Takal is still uncertain given its experimental nature, but I have absolute faith that it will work as designed."

Reynolds grinned broadly. "I'd kiss you if I didn't think it would fry my circuits."

"A simple thanks will suffice," the alien protested.

The AI spun away from the alien as the Gulg ships

ganged up on one of the enemy destroyers and took it down.

"There we go," he said, then triggered the comm. "Time's up, Takal. Put your baby to work."

"As you wish," Takal replied.

"Pull us out of the fight, Ensign," Reynolds ordered as the ship was targeted by Phraim-'Eh's *Godhand*.

The ship trembled, and Reynolds could feel the blow to his core as Ria raced to comply with his order.

"Shields at twenty percent." Asya wiped sweat from her brow, eyes narrowed as she both commanded the superdreadnought and kept track of all the damage reports as they whirled across her monitor.

"Can we buffer them again?" Reynolds questioned.

"Not if we want to keep the ESD in reserve," she replied matter-of-factly. "We'll end up trading one for another if we go that route."

"I can help a little with that," Xyxl told them, "but it won't be much. My own energies are depleted from the journey here."

Reynolds nodded. "We'll make do," he said.

The *Godhand* pulled back as the three Gulg ships went after it. Bursts of energy trailed after it, tearing at its shields, then the massive ship swung about and returned fire.

Reynolds didn't see what happened because a destroyer filled his view then. It opened up, and the SD *Reynolds* bucked under the assault.

Then it was over and the destroyer was veering off, its lower hull shrieking past not twenty meters above the superdreadnought as Takal's and Xyxl's program took hold of the ship and usurped its command just as Jora'nal had done to Gorad's and the Gulg ships.

"Holy Fuck!" Jiya cheered.

"It works!" Takal shouted over the comm. "It truly works. I'm in complete control of the craft."

"I knew it would," Reynolds told him.

He caught Jiya grilling him with a raised eyebrow.

"Okay, I'll admit...I really *wanted* it to work," he clarified.

Jiya chuckled.

But even with Takal and Xyxl's secret project having borne fruit, the *Reynolds* wasn't out of danger.

Two more of the destroyers maneuvered into position and pounded the ship.

The bridge went dark, then the emergency lights fluttered and came on. The crew were cast in deep shadows.

"Shields at twelve percent, Captain," Asya reported. "One or two more hits and we'll be counting on the armor alone," she warned.

Takal's controlled destroyer streaked past them again, crashing headlong into the first of the two destroyers chasing the superdreadnought.

There was a thunderous boom when they collided and the two ships spun away, forever entangled.

"One of the Gulg ships dropped off the scanners," Asya told the AI, casting a furtive glance Xyxl's direction.

"My people transferred to the next ship in line, so don't worry for us," the alien assured them.

"That is such a neat trick," Jiya commented.

"It has its benefits, no doubt," Xyxl agreed.

"What's the count, Asya?" Reynolds asked.

"Four, not counting your half a ship, which still hasn't rejoined the fight," she replied.

"Three if you remove the one I've just taken control of," Takal crowed. "Though I have to admit, these ships are quite difficult to maneuver."

The *Reynolds* was struck from behind, weapons fire strafing its length as Ria dodged to avoid the full impact.

"*Godhand* is on our ass," Asya said.

"That's a bit perverse," Ka'nak said from the back of the bridge.

"My companions are on it," Xyxl assured, but the super-dreadnought ended up on the receiving end of yet another blast of fire.

"Shields are fucked, Captain. Cooked," Asya told the AI. "All that stands between them and us is the armor."

Two of the remaining destroyers tag-teamed one of the Gulg ships, slipping around behind it while it engaged the *Godhand*.

Its hull was ripped open at its flank, and although it wasn't a killing blow, the ship had no choice but to veer aside and break off its pursuit of Phraim-'Eh's command ship.

Takal released control of the ship he had previously grabbed after shooting it off into space, and he took the reins of one of the destroyers that had just wounded the Gulg ship.

That ship spun on its companion and opened up at close range. The targeted ship's shields flashed, but most of the blasts struck true, blowing through its defenses.

The wounded destroyer listed, lost control, and began to tumble. It collided with one of the few remaining patches of cloaked mines, which only compounded its misery.

It tumbled end over end and disappeared into the blackness of space.

"Can you grab the damn *Godhand*?" Reynolds asked the inventor as the monstrous ship recovered from the Gulg attack. It reengaged the *Reynolds* after a destroyer assailed the last of the functional Gulg craft and peeled it off the *Godhand*'s back.

"We're not going to win the fight like this," Reynold said more to himself than anyone else. "We've got to do something different."

He glanced at Jiya, wondering what she would do in that situation, and it came to him.

Something crazy.

"Coordinate with me, Xyxl," the AI called. "Ria, bring us about as sharply as you can without ripping us in half."

The ensign did just that. The ship felt as if it might tear apart at the seams, but it held. "Tactical, hit that asshole with everything we've got left right where I'm marking the target."

He spun on the alien.

"Have your ship do the same, Xyxl," he urged. "Fuck it! You too, Takal. Put that borrowed muscle to work."

All three ships converged on the *Godhand*, angling around to come at it from the same side. Accidentally obliging them, the command ship turned away to avoid a possible collision, only to mistakenly give them an easier target.

The trio of ships fired within milliseconds of one

another, each blast crashing into the *Godhand*'s shields at almost exactly the same spot.

To disastrous effect.

A ripple formed in the enemy's shield and it ran outward, the combined attacks tearing a hole in the *Godhand*'s defenses.

Reynolds knew it would only last for a moment.

"Ka'nak, Jiya, on me," Reynolds called.

Though they had no idea what he was summoning them for, both crewmembers raced over to his side by instinct, eyes wide, questioning what he expected of them.

Reynolds overrode the transport system and sent them hurtling across space toward the rip in the *Godhand*'s shields.

The three of them crashed to the deck aboard Phraim-'Eh's command ship, having appeared about a foot off the ground.

Every cultist on the bridge turned and stared at them, disbelieving and frozen in place.

"A little warning next time," Jiya said as she scrambled to her feet, unholstered her pistol, and started shooting cultists. "How'd you even know where to place us?"

Ka'nak didn't even bother to grab his weapon. He plowed into the cultists wholesale and began beating them to death before they even realized what was happening.

"I scanned the layout of one of Phraim-'Eh's destroyers," the AI explained. "They and the command ship are quite similar in external design, especially when it comes to the forward nose and bridge area. I made an educated guess as to where we would land." Reynolds raised a finger. "Oh, by the way, Asya, you've got the conn," Reynolds called into his comm.

Asya chuckled across the connection. "Better late than never, right?"

Reynolds spun around and blasted a cultist who'd found the presence of mind to draw his pistol. He crumpled to the floor, dead.

Not having expected the sudden arrival of the enemy on their command ship's bridge, the cultists fell into disarray and died quickly.

Ka'nak stretched his moment out a little longer, swinging a cultist in each hand to bash their brethren to death with their bodies. Blood was flung across consoles and pooled on the deck around him.

"I think they're dead now," Jiya told him.

The Melowi glanced from his right hand to his left, seeing both of the bodies there hanging limp.

"So they are," he replied, shrugging and tossing the corpses aside.

Jiya turned to look at Reynolds. "What now?"

"Start breaking shit," he ordered, taking the lead and blasting the nearest console.

"That's my kind of order." Ka'nak grinned and started to smashing anything he could get his hands on.

Jiya followed suit, choosing to shoot the command consoles first, hoping to disable the ship to keep it from being used against the SD *Reynolds* and her friends.

"You dare!" A loud, gravelly voice screeched from the open doorway.

The crew spun around to see Phraim-'Eh standing there, nearly frothing at the mouth in his rage.

Reynolds went to respond, but the would-be god was far faster than the AI anticipated.

He was across the bridge in two leaping steps, and he crashed into Reynolds' android body, the two of them slamming into the nearest console.

The impact shook the deck.

Reynolds reeled as he tried to comprehend the speed and power of Phraim-'Eh. It was nearly unfathomable.

Sensors noted that his uniform had been ripped open and the faux flesh on his back has been sliced off by the sharp edge of the console. Servos whined in his spine, and warning lights flickered in his vision.

Reynolds couldn't ever remember having been struck that hard.

And Phraim-'Eh had only begun.

He lifted Reynolds into the air and slammed him to the deck as if he were a doll in the hands of a giant.

There was a sharp snap, and the AI realized his mechanical arm had popped at the joint and was angled backward, opposite its normal direction.

His mind reeled under the onslaught, and he watched as the god pulled back a fist and made ready to smash his face in.

Jiya got there first.

She stepped up, far too close to Phraim-'Eh Reynolds realized, and shot him dead center in his chest.

The cultists' god was flung backward, colliding with a wall and sliding to the floor. Reynolds dropped, but Jiya caught him by his stable arm and wrenched him back to his feet.

"You shouldn't have done that," Reynolds told her.

"Like I'm going to leave you to get your ass kicked," she said, grinning. "Not even if he is a god."

"Watch out!" Ka'nak yelled.

Phraim-'Eh was on his feet already, and he lunged at Reynolds and Jiya. She turned her weapon on the god, but Ka'nak plowed into him first. The two crashed to the floor in a mass of tangled, thrashing limbs.

"Stay away from him," Reynolds warned. "He's too strong."

Ka'nak learned that the hard way.

Phraim-'Eh shrugged the brawler off with ease and drove a fist into the Melowi's sternum. A sharp crack told Reynolds something had been broken inside Ka'nak.

The warrior screamed, but he was made of far sterner stuff than even Reynolds realized.

He gritted his teeth and ignored the pain, driving a brutal punch into Phraim-'Eh's kidney, followed by a second.

The blows lifted the would-be god off his feet.

Ka'nak came around with a wide right hook to follow up. Knuckles collided with the hard bone of the god's jaw, and another *pop* reverberated through the room.

Phraim-'Eh stumbled backward from the impact, eyes narrowed and steeped with pain.

Despite the perfectly targeted punch, a quick glance at Ka'nak's misshapen fist told the AI that he hadn't delivered the blow without consequence.

But if a broken hand meant anything to the Melowi, it wasn't clear.

He leaped across the intervening space between him and Phraim-'Eh and punched him in the face again and again and again with his already-damaged fist.

The blows drove Phraim-'Eh to one knee, but there was plenty of fight left in him.

Ka'nak had to lean over to continue punching him, so he slammed his forehead into the Melowi's face and shattered the warrior's nose. A gush of blood spewed forth and washed across his mouth and chin like a waterfall.

Ka'nak stumbled, his legs wobbling beneath him, but Jiya jumped back into the fight.

She scorched a trail of fire up Phraim-'Eh's body, starting at his belly and shooting her way up until she blasted him in the face.

The would-be god rolled with the last of the shots and howled as he staggered to the side.

Reynolds wouldn't let him off the hook.

The AI charged the god and kicked him against the wall, using the momentum of Phraim-'Eh bouncing back to drive his good fist into the god's throat.

Phraim-'Eh gasped and clutched his neck, gurgles and froth spilling from his mouth as he struggled to breathe.

Reynolds struck him again, metallic fist colliding with the sharpened ledge of his cheek, shattering the bone there with a sound like kindling snapped apart.

Phraim-'Eh snarled and backhanded Reynolds, driving him back several steps, but the AI stayed on his feet.

Phraim-'Eh roared, "I will slay you all!"

He bounded forward and crashed into Reynolds again.

A vicious punch to the android's side bent several of his ribs. A second blow bent them inside, and Reynolds felt the metal framework of his body grinding hard against its internal workings.

Phraim-'Eh's third punch definitely destroyed something.

Reynolds coughed and spit out a mouthful of greasy oil. It dribbled down his chest as the god drew back his hand to strike Reynolds again.

"You're starting to piss me off," Jiya told him as she unloaded her gun into Phraim-'Eh's spine.

He stumbled forward, ranting and raving, clawing at his wounds as he darted sideways to step behind cover.

Jiya reloaded.

Ka'nak stepped out of nowhere and drove his good fist into Phraim-'Eh's nose, adding shattered cartilage to the orbital injury he was already nursing.

Phraim-'Eh shoved the warrior aside and managed to step away just as Jiya found a good angle and lit him up. Several rounds grazed the wannabe god as he circled around a console and came at Reynolds again.

"This is all because of you," he screamed. "I will tear down your Federation and burn everything you hold dear to the ground. I am a god, and you will kneel before your better!"

Phraim-'Eh crashed into Reynolds again and drove his back into a wall. The bridge shuddered under the impact.

"Die, android! Die!" he shouted over and over as he pistoned blows into Reynolds head, neck, and torso.

Reynolds' vision blurred and began blackening at the edges, his sight beginning to tunnel.

Fuck this!

Pressed against the wall, Reynolds could barely move, but he sure as fuck wasn't going to sit there and let this asshole beat him into so much scrap.

The AI fought back, trading blow for blow with his one good arm, but there was no doubt he was losing the war of attrition. His mechanical body would give out before Phraim-'Eh's would.

"You are nothing!" the god screamed. "I am a *god*!"

As Reynolds suffered under the hail of brutal punches, he caught sight of his broken arm flapping at his side.

It looked almost comical as it waved like a banner in high winds, whipping all over.

"You will die! I. Am. A. God!"

Reynolds growled and spat oil in Phraim' Eh's face.

"Seriously, shut the…" he started.

He reached down and grabbed his flapping arm with his good hand. Reynolds yanked hard, ripping the limp appendage from the rest of his frame. Then he maneuvered the broken arm around and stuffed the forearm into Phraim-'Eh's mouth.

"…fuck up!" Reynolds finished.

Phraim-'Eh snarled around the mechanical limb in his mouth, but he couldn't shake it free without releasing Reynolds.

Which was what the AI was looking for him to do, but Jiya had other plans.

"A hand, please," she called.

For a second, Reynolds thought she was being a smartass, referencing the mangled arm stuffed in Phraim-'Eh's mouth, but his confusion only lasted for a second.

She and Ka'nak came to stand at Phraim-'Eh's back.

Enveloped in his rage, the would-be god didn't even notice.

At least not until Ka'nak locked his hands on both sides of the arm stuck in the god's mouth.

He grunted a muffled, "What..." but that was all he managed to get out before the Melowi dropped all his weight on the android arm and pulled down.

Phraim-'Eh's eyes shot wide as his jaw stretched, all of Ka'nak's weight and strength yanking it downward.

There was a moment of resistance, then the would-be god's jaw snapped on both sides, the bone stretching the tendons hanging loosely in front of his neck.

All resistance gone, Ka'nak fell to the deck with Reynolds' arm still in his hands, blood and spittle everywhere.

Phraim-'Eh stumbled back a step, his grip on Reynolds lost.

That was when Jiya moved up beside him and stuffed a small, round, metal device in the wannabe god's gaping mouth.

"*Now* it's grenade time," the first officer told Ka'nak as he sat there gathering his strength.

Phraim-'Eh realized then what Jiya had stuffed in his mouth. He gurgled and reached to yank it loose, but Reynolds was quicker.

He drove his metallic stump up under Phraim-'Eh's mangled chin and forced his mouth shut around the grenade.

With his good hand, he grabbed Phraim-'Eh's hair and spun him around, kicking out his feet. Phraim-'Eh toppled forward, and Reynolds helped him down. The would-be deity slammed face-first into the hard steel of the deck, muffled shrieks spilling from him the entire time.

He squirmed and thrashed and fought, but Reynolds held him still, grinding his face into the deck so hard his every shout vibrated the deck.

"You are no god," Reynolds told Phraim-'Eh.

And then he was nothing.

The grenade exploded, taking Phraim-'Eh's head with it.

Reynolds didn't even turn away.

He wanted to witness every instant of Phraim-'Eh's death.

It wasn't until the body stopped squirming that he let go and straightened, the servos in his back squealing.

"That...was fucking gross," Jiya said, letting out a muted chuckle as she wiped her face.

Reynolds went over and helped Ka'nak to his feet.

As the three stood there gathering their wits, a sharp snarl came across the comm.

"If you three are done playing around over there, we could use your help," Asya barked.

CHAPTER TWENTY-ONE

Takal transported the trio back to the *Reynolds*, and the crew stared at them wide-eyed, seeing the condition they were in.

Reynolds assessed the situation and waved off their concerned offers to help.

"There's no time," he told them, waving Asya back to her seat.

Despite the *Godhand* being disabled, the last two destroyers had yet to relent.

All of the Gulg ships had been destroyed. The only craft left was the *Reynolds*, but it was little more than a heap of battered steel after all it had been through.

Shields gone, its armor had been chipped away at by the remaining cultist ships, and nothing remained of its ammo save for a few thousand railgun rounds. Those would be chewed up in moments.

"You didn't happen to bring a magic wand back with you, did you?" Tactical asked.

"I wish," Jiya replied. "We have any Pods left?"

"A couple, but we've been throwing those at the destroyers ever since we ran out of missiles," Asya told her.

"Pucks, mines?" Jiya pressed.

"Some loose ones out there somewhere." Asya gestured in the general direction of space.

"Can you and your people power us up?" Reynolds asked Xyxl.

The pale, ghostly alien shook his head. "I'm afraid not. We've been sustaining the last of the shields and allowing your pilot enough power to continue evading, but even that will soon come to an end."

"What about yours and Takal's program?"

"There was a flaw in the coding," Xyxl admitted. "While we had success early on, with each successive attempt, it became harder to control the enemy craft. We are unable to access their programming at all now."

"Gate drive's out too, before you ask," Asya reported.

"Then we're left with one last option," Reynold said.

"That ship has sailed, buddy," Tactical told him. "We ramp up the ESD now, and none of us are walking away from this. It won't be a victory, it will be a glorious tie."

The ship jumped as the destroyers closed, every blow tearing the life from the superdreadnought.

Reynolds reached into the ship with his senses and felt for his personalities, felt for every wire, every conduit and circuit, every electrical charge.

The ship was spent.

"No," he said, shaking his head. "I refuse to surrender. I refuse to die and let even two of these fucking ships get away."

He turned to face the crew. "Everyone strap in. We're not going down without a fight."

Jiya nodded and went to her station. Ka'nak followed, and Geroux and Maddox buckled in a moment later.

"Let's kick their asses," Jiya said.

Reynolds offered her the best smile his mangled face could manage, and he motioned to Tactical with his one good hand.

"Fire up the ESD."

To his surprise, Tactical didn't bother to argue.

As the weapon warmed up, Xyxl and his crewmates down in the bowels of the ship providing the ship with as much energy as they could bear to part with, Reynolds eased into the captain's chair.

The enemy destroyers hammered at them all the while, each blow chipping away at the armored hull and bringing them closer to destruction.

Reynolds sank into his seat, both mentally and physically.

The part of him that was the ship hummed in the background, growing louder and more powerful with every passing second. He reached into the ship, dove into it and drew it in, welcoming back the solid steel structure that had been his home for so long.

It was as if he were adrift on the ocean, the waves carrying him, buoying his essence as he connected with the hulk that was him once more.

Earlier, he'd stepped away from the ship, severed the link and tasted what he had believed was freedom.

He'd been wrong.

Being separated from the ship, from himself, was not freedom. It was torture.

No matter how much he wanted the experience of walking upright and appearing humanoid, in the end, he was who he was.

The ship.

It was him, as he was it.

There was no separating them on a molecular level. They would always be one.

But he'd learned many lessons while he'd been mobile, the greatest of which was perseverance.

There were still too many things he wanted to experience, to take part in, to feel, so he found it impossible to give in and accept defeat if it meant he would fail himself, fail Bethany Anne or, most of all, fail his crew.

All their trials had led them here, to this moment, and he would use his strength to overcome.

"Bring us about!" he ordered, his voice ethereal, barely above a whisper. He realized it came both from his mouth and the speakers built into his flesh in the ceiling above.

Ria obeyed and swung him around.

He could feel her hands on his controls, sense the anticipation and excitement in her grip. She moved him instinctively, and he gave in to her, letting her have complete control.

A rumbling in his center drew him through the system; a gnawing, burning hunger that seared his guts.

He followed the feeling deeper and deeper into himself. He slithered through the channels he had designed to protect him from the ravaging power spewed from within.

It was like riding a volcano in reverse, diving down into

the cone and fighting the flow of lava as it fought to dislodge him, spit him out.

Reynolds wasn't going anywhere.

He doubled-down and pushed harder, at last coming to the source of the scalding, searing sun that churned and bubbled, its energies growing harder and harder to contain.

The view was mesmerizing.

He stared at it, watch the power grow and expand until it was ready to overflow.

Somewhere deep inside himself, he knew he had come there for something, to do something, but he didn't know what. He couldn't remember.

And the power started to spill over.

He touched it, and sharp agony fired through him.

It was then that he remembered why he was there, what he had to do.

Some piece of himself that sat in the captain's chair recalled his purpose. It drew him back from oblivion.

It's the pain. That's why I'm drifting.

Reynolds spat his defiance at the agony that threatened to consume him, and he remembered the enemy ships he was facing down.

The ones that wanted to kill him.

No!

His voice roared, and he rode it out alongside the gushing energy. Blackness appeared ahead, a circle of emptiness that grew larger with every passing instant.

It hurtled toward him as he rode the energy upward toward the enveloping darkness.

That same voice that had summoned him back from the

edge warned him about the darkness, warned him away from it.

It was a place for the light, not for him.

His job was to see the light to the end of its passage within him, and then let it go.

So that was what he did.

At the very edge of the tunnel, he braced against the walls, clutched himself, and held tight.

The raging energy spilled past him, tearing, tugging, desperately trying to drag him along, but he resisted. He wouldn't give in to its pull.

He clung to himself as great tremors rattled through his frame, trying to shake him apart.

Reynolds hung on because he knew Bethany Anne would want him to. Because he knew people were counting on him.

Because he needed to.

At that moment, he was everything and nothing at the same time.

Still, the energy clawed at him, trying to drag him along.

Reynolds denied it.

He screamed his defiance into the rage of the energy surging past him, and he felt it give way and weaken.

It had bowed to his will, and then it was gone.

Spent.

And so was he.

Yet he still held on.

The next thing Reynolds knew, he was back in the android body he'd been sporting for the past several months.

Battered and beaten, missing a limb and barely able to walk, he smiled as he settled in again.

He blinked to clear his vision and saw the crew standing around him, eyes wide with wonder. They saw his motion, and smiles rippled across their faces.

"There's no place like home," he said, letting his head loll back against the headrest for a second.

"Are you okay?" Jiya asked, gaze darting about, examining every inch of him.

He nodded, straightening in his seat.

"I'm okay," he told her, easing his neck from side to side while listening to the squeaks of its motion. "I might be about a quart of oil low, though."

Jiya laughed, and the crew crowded tighter around, murmuring platitudes and saying how glad they were he'd made it through everything.

That touchy-feely shit lasted all of two seconds.

"Get the fuck back to work, you slackers," Reynolds ordered. "I don't pay all of you to hang around and grease my wheels. Man your stations, and tell me what the fuck-all happened while I was riding the LSD trip up my asshole. And get rid of Phraim-'Eh's fucking flagship, while you're at it. Might as well take out all of the trash before we leave."

"Good to have you back, Captain," Asya remarked.

"Good to *be* back," he replied. "Now, someone track down Takal and tell him I need a tune-up. And a new arm."

EPILOGUE ONE

Jiya stood on the corner, staring down the street as though she were watching the parade roll by like all the other people gathered there on a quiet holiday morning in the sleepy city of Augst.

She wasn't, of course.

She'd been stationed there to keep an eye out for the Voice, or as they'd learned, his real name was Commander Ast, and he was from the same world as Asya, a Loranian.

That had been a real kick in the ass to find out.

Asya had even worked for him for a time.

She'd damn near flown into a rage once she realized Ast had been the reason for Reynolds' earlier mistrust of her. The male had manipulated everything, giving the AI cause to doubt her loyalty before she'd proven herself.

All that just pissed Jiya off even more.

It was one thing to stalk the crew across the universe and try to murder them, it was something else entirely to betray Jiya's friend and use the crew.

He'd been behind everything from the very first mission, Phraim-'Eh's eyes and ears...

Jiya laughed about that.

He'd have to be now, seeing how the wannabe god didn't have eyes or ears anymore, or nose or mouth or anything now that his head had been blown off.

Jiya wanted to do the same thing to Commander Ast, but so did Asya and the rest of the crew.

They'd worked it out that the first person who found him got to put a bullet in his head.

It'd become a bit of a competition.

Now, nearly three months later, the crew had figured out where he'd been hiding since they'd killed all the rest of the Phraim-'Eh cultists that had scattered across the universe.

He'd vanished as soon as he'd learned that Phraim-'Eh was dead.

Jiya couldn't blame him, but she sure as shit didn't have any sympathy for the guy. He was a dead Loranian walking, and she wanted him found and taken out sooner rather than later. He'd been free far too long as far as she was concerned.

The chatter of the crowd threatened to lull her to sleep with its tepid pitch as she casually used her peripheral vision and her suit's computer systems to scan each and every face that came anywhere near her. Every whispered "ooh" and "aah" gave her reason to glance around and scan even further.

She hadn't been lucky enough to catch sight of him, though, and she was beginning to think they'd followed bad intel.

"Anyone see him?" Ka'nak asked.

"Would we tell you if we did?" Maddox answered.

"The mission is what matters, people," Reynolds said over the comm. "And I'll let you know if I spot him...right after I scoop his fucking brains off the sidewalk."

"You are all much too competitive," Geroux told them.

"You're not exactly immune to it," Jiya fired back. "I saw how much computer equipment you packed when we heard he was down here. You took half the damn ship with you just so you can find him first."

"It's for the team," Geroux retorted.

"Is that why I'm stuck using my suit scanners while you've rigged up half the city's security cams and sent out a horde of mini-drones?" Jiya asked.

"See how helpful I am?" The young tech laughed.

"Keep it down, people," Asya told the crew. "I can't hear myself think with all your chatter, let alone concentrate enough to find that bastard."

"Someone's cranky," Ka'nak chided.

"I think I see him," Maddox interrupted.

"Where?" the rest of the crew asked simultaneously.

Maddox chuckled across the comm, saying nothing.

Jiya really didn't care who got him. She just wanted to be sure that he was caught and put down.

Every other true cultist with the exception of Jora'nal had been killed, and that bastard was in jail on Lariest, where he'd rot in a cell forever alongside her father.

It was kind of a fitting ending for both of them, and she hoped the two were locked up close enough to piss each other off regularly.

That thought gave her great satisfaction.

A flurry of movement against the flow of pedestrian traffic caught her attention, and Jiya cast a furtive glance that way.

And there he was.

Her heart raced, and she almost hit her comm and pointed him out, but as much as it wasn't about the competition, she needed to see the job through.

This guy had made a fool out of all of them.

Jiya relaxed and sucked in a cool, deep breath to calm her nerves, then she leaned against the wall, turning her face away so he couldn't recognize her.

He glanced at the crowd, then ducked into a narrow alley off the main street the parade traversed.

Jiya eased behind the crowds, their good-natured pushing and shoving nearly pressing her against the shops that lined the street. She dodged both vendors and sightseers as she wound her way toward the alley he'd gone down.

She didn't want to trigger her cloaking device, since the rest of the crew would know she had and would come running. That would be a sure sign she'd spotted him.

Jiya reached the corner of the alley and eased to the edge, stepping off the curb and daring a peek around.

She nearly lost her head for it.

A burst of gunfire tore apart the bricks just inches above where her head had been. He'd apparently misjudged her height, thanks to the curb.

The crowd reacted to the shot, all hell breaking loose.

Children started crying, and people started screaming and wailing, and the thunder of footsteps of those who were part of the parade and those watching it joined into a singular cacophony.

"Where did that come from?" Reynolds asked over the comm.

Jiya resisted answering, but the question had come from her superior. It was instinct to reply.

"Small alley by Wallaths grocery," she answered, knowing the rest of the crew would be breathing down her neck in seconds.

She dropped low and sprinted down the alley.

Of course, Ast had already bolted out the other side.

"He's loose on the street parallel to the parade course," she reported. "And I better get a damn raise for being a team player."

She skidded around the corner just as Commander Ast made the next one. Jiya recognized the vague outline of his attire before he disappeared.

Without hesitation, she continued the chase.

She wasn't alone.

Asya thundered up on her heels and the two wordlessly followed, Asya drafting off Jiya's lead.

Ast hit a straight patch and was forced to press hard to find cover while he ran. He darted left to right, bobbing and weaving to avoid being hit in the back. Asya gave it her best shot, though.

Blaster fire illuminated the alley and scored the walls around the runner, but he was fast and unpredictable, and Asya hit everything but him.

"You're going to bring the police down on us," Jiya warned.

Asya did her best to shrug while running. "Like him shooting into a crowd hasn't already set that in motion?"

She had a point.

"North on Clatterdun," Jiya reported as Ast skittered and darted right down a side street.

"On him," Maddox called.

"Damn it, Jiya," Asya bitched at her friend. "If he gets to him before me because you're calling the chase, I swear…"

She let the threat hang, but Jiya had a pretty good idea what Asya was willing to do.

Honor was a big thing to her, much as it was with Bethany Anne.

Asya might not have the same sense of absolute Justice in the face of any and all circumstances, but she sure as hell did everything she could to avenge a slight against her *or* her friends.

"East on Malfar," Geroux reported, growling at herself when she realized she had given up Ast's location freely. "Damn it! Now you've got *me* doing it, Jiya."

Jiya and Asya shifted course to intercept, letting Maddox burn his energy in the sprint to catch up.

"He's coming back toward you, Jiya," Ka'nak called.

Ast popped out of a side alley not more than twenty seconds later. He skidded to a halt in the middle of a four-way cross-section as he saw Asya and Jiya, believing he had given them the slip.

Since that was clearly not the case, he raised his gun, but both Asya and Jiya fired first.

Ast ducked and spun back around, just barely missing colliding with Ka'nak, who barreled out of the easternmost alley.

Maddox appeared and blocked the way he'd just come, so Ast spun again—and ran face-first into the barrel of Geroux's extended pistol.

He winced and stumbled back, regaining his footing and raising his gun to shoot his way out.

The problem was that he was surrounded on all four sides.

Actually, five, since Reynolds appeared on one of the rooftops, whistling down at Commander Ast as he aimed a rifle at him.

"Today is not your day, Ast," Asya told him. "Or do you prefer 'Voice of Phraim-'Eh?'"

"I find that last one a bit gaudy," Geroux admitted as she inched closer, leaving Ast no room to run around her without guaranteeing he got shot.

"You know your god's dead, right?" Ka'nak asked him, then mimicked a grenade going off. "Boom! God bits *everywhere*."

Commander Ast snarled, spinning in a desperate circle.

"Come on now, Voice, you have to have something to say," Jiya told him. "I mean, it's right there in the name and everything."

"Just take me in," Ast argued. "I'll go peacefully." He moved like he was going to set his weapon down.

"Oh, no, no, no. That will not do," Asya taunted. "We're past the point of you surrendering and earning yourself a comfy prison cell. No, we're taking care of this here and now."

"You're not murderers," he told them. "You won't kill me in cold blood."

Ka'nak chuckled. "You might have us mistaken for someone else."

Jiya appreciated the Melowi's bluster, but Ast was right; they *weren't* murderers. They weren't looking to gun down a person in cold blood, regardless of the crimes he'd committed.

But that certainly didn't stop them from pushing to make sure the killer in Ast came out so it could be punished properly.

The crew inched closer, guns up and at the ready. Reynolds covered them from above.

"A bunch of people died because of you, Ast," Asya explained. "You don't just get to walk away from that. There's blood on your hands. Innocent blood, and lots of it."

"I was simply a servant of my god," he pleaded.

Asya laughed in his face. "Pathetic. He wasn't even a god. You were schlepping drinks and running errands for a pretender. A crackpot."

"He wasn't worthy of calling himself sentient, let alone a god," Maddox pressed.

The gun in Ast's hand trembled as he spun in slow circles, facing the crew and their judgment.

"The sound of his jaw snapping is something I'll remember forever," Ka'nak said.

Ast twisted to glare at the Melowi, but Asya's words caught him cold.

"He died crying," she said. "Did you know that? Your god wept and pleaded for his life before his head exploded."

"No!" Ast shrieked and turned, bringing his gun up and pulling the trigger.

His shot went wide.

Asya put a smoking hole between his eyes and killed him right there.

The rest of the crew fired right after, each claiming their right to Justice for what he'd done.

Commander Ast, the Voice of Phraim-'Eh, stood in the middle of a dingy alley, a corpse already, but his body too stubborn to realize it.

He held his ground with rigid defiance, then crumpled to the ground in a heap, nothing more than a bad memory like his would-be god, Phraim-'Eh.

The crew lingered for a while, not moving, simply staring at the end of their mission lying dead on the ground.

"Okay, people, let's wrap this shit up," Reynolds called from the rooftop. "He got his, now it's time to move on."

The crew nodded and put their guns away, glancing around the group. Small smiles crept to their lips.

Yeah, they'd killed someone, but he'd fucking deserved it.

"Six to beam up, Scotty," Reynolds called to the *Reynolds*. "And a corpse. Don't forget the corpse. We can't just leave that in the gutter like some Old West movie."

Takal came back over the comm, "Who is this Scotty you keep bringing up? Did we hire someone new?"

EPILOGUE TWO

The mission was over.

At least this part of it, Reynolds thought.

He and the crew had come through it all and had taken out the evil descendants of the Kurtherians who had invaded the Chain Galaxy, and who had hoped to expand beyond even that.

And they'd killed a god.

Well, not really a god. More like a delusional nutbag who'd managed to get his hands on corrupt nanocytes somewhere and juiced himself into an early grave.

He'd convinced a lot of people, though, and had brought a lot of bad shit down on good worlds.

Reynolds was proud to have taken part in helping those worlds recover. Him and his crew.

They'd been a big part of it, regardless of how shaky their start had been. He couldn't have done it without them.

It was also nice to have the last leader of the cult dead and accounted for.

Now that he was fully recovered—Takal having rebuilt his body and the crew having repaired the ship, making them both whole—it was time to make a decision.

Reynolds sat the core crew down in the meeting room and used the audio-video system to project his message to the entire ship.

He felt it only fair to tell them what he intended and give them a choice.

He sat at the head of the table and looked out across the closest of his crew. Reynolds dreaded this moment, but like every other circle of life, it begins and it ends, and it isn't entirely up to us when it happens.

"Given that my mission here is over, the Kurtherians I sought vanquished, I figure this would be as good a time as any to clear the air and see what the future holds and what roles you play in it.

"I've enjoyed spending time with each and every one of you, and our experiences will forever be locked in up here…" he tapped the side of his head, "but I feel I have to be honest with you.

"I really don't know where I'm going from here," he admitted. "I'm thinking I'll travel to High Tortuga to resolve a personal issue, but that's not a guarantee."

He purposely didn't mention Bethany Anne or the Federation so as to avoid feeling as though he were manipulating or coercing decisions from people.

"There's no real direction set for me right now, since I'll always be chasing Kurtherians wherever they appear. It doesn't feel right to drag all of you along without some certainty somewhere along the way."

Reynolds paused and looked at the crew in front of

him. They sat without saying a word, which was what he had expected. Thanks to being the ship, he could hear the muttered conversations of the entire crew, no matter where they were, although he blocked them out for the time being.

He didn't want to get a false sense of things by eaves-dropping and pushing for something they really didn't want. Reynolds wanted a truly independent decision on behalf of the crew.

"Anyway, I'll come out and say it. I'm leaving on an adventure to who knows where, for who knows how long, with who knows what outcome. So...who wants in?"

He waited quietly as the crew made up their minds.

The answer wasn't long in coming.

"We've decided we're going with you, Reynolds," Jiya told him. "Someone's got to be there to clean up all your shit."

Thank you for reading this book, and you're still reading! Oorah, hard-chargers. I really hope you liked this story.

The readers have spoken! So many people were disappointed to hear that Superdreadnought would wrap up with number 5, but it won't. We will continue the series with a big shake-up for Book 6 (not the core of the crew, but where they are and where they're going). Thank you for being polite and vocal in your need for more Superdreadnought. You are the reason I do what I do. We have the stories left to tell, so we'll tell them. For you.

I spent the last week in sunny Wisconsin. I'm being sarcastic. I left beautiful temperatures that had finally made it above freezing (we went 114 days straight without a high above freezing this year – that's far from a record in

Fairbanks, Alaska), but it wasn't in Wisconsin. I watched temps climb where I live close to the Arctic Circle while they plunged in Wisconsin. It took almost the full week before temps were above freezing. And when they did climb past 32F all the way to 34, it started raining, like a total downpour rain.

Then temps returned to the low 20s. Sweet. At least when the sun hit the next day, it melted most of the ice and dried up the roads. Wisconsin.

I was there for a gaming convention, more fantasy gaming and that kind of stuff, a bunch of older folks who were introduced to Dungeons and Dragons in the 1970s now have a convention every year around Gary Gygax's birthday to celebrate a life well-played.

That was a long week. I was tired constantly from so much peopling, but it was good and I like the people who attend that show. I had a lot of great conversations with people who are important to me. I also got to spend a great deal of time with my brother, not something I take for granted nowadays. He lost his wife of forty years back in October. I've talked with him more on the phone and spent more time with him in the past six months than I had in the previous ten years.

I spent a lot of last year's latter half getting books ready to storm 2019:) I have a few series that are doing exceptionally well and a couple, not so much. Sometimes, I have no idea why one series will resonate more with readers than another, but no matter what, I do my best to make sure they are well written. That is in my control. I like the latest reviews on Judge, Jury, & Executioner 5 – <u>Slave Trade</u>, a book that made its appearance a week ago.

Five Stars! An exceptionally well written, fast paced, action filled book. The characters are well developed and the story held my attention and demanded that I finish it in one sitting. Looking forward to the next book in this series.

Five Stars! I recommend this series it has colorful characters and is very entertaining. I also like the way characters from the rest of the universe make occasional appearances.

Those kind words keep the fires stoked within and make me keep striving for better and better. I hope you like what you read in Superdreadnought 5. It is a nice piece of work that I think you'll enjoy.

We've worked through the details of *Superdreadnought 6*'s outline to come up with a great transition story. No more plot reveals at this point. I am a ways into Bad Company 5 – Destroyer and will dabble on that each day to try and finish the story by the end of March. That will give me a nice leg up for April.

Back to the word mines to find those golden nuggets for you.

Peace, fellow humans.

Please join my Newsletter (www.craigmartelle.com – please, please, please sign up!), or you can follow me on Facebook since you'll get the same opportunity to pick up the books for only 99 cents on that first Saturday after they are published.

If you liked this story, you might like some of my other

books. You can join my mailing list by dropping by my website www.craigmartelle.com, or if you have any comments, shoot me a note at craig@craigmartelle.com. I am always happy to hear from people who've read my work. I try to answer every email I receive.

If you liked the story, please write a short review for me on Amazon. I greatly appreciate any kind words. Even one or two sentences go a long way. The number of reviews an ebook receives greatly improves how well it does on Amazon.

Amazon – www.amazon.com/author/craigmartelle

BookBub – https://www.bookbub.com/authors/craig-martelle

Facebook – www.facebook.com/authorcraigmartelle

My web page – www.craigmartelle.com

That's it—break's over, back to writing the next book.

Craig Martelle's other books (listed by series)

For a complete list of books from Craig, please see www.craigmartelle.com

Terry Henry Walton Chronicles (co-written with Michael Anderle) – a post-apocalyptic paranormal adventure

Gateway to the Universe (co-written with Justin Sloan & Michael Anderle) – this book transitions the characters from the Terry Henry Walton Chronicles to The Bad Company

The Bad Company (co-written with Michael Anderle) – a military science fiction space opera

End Times Alaska (also available in audio) – a Permuted Press publication – a post-apocalyptic survivalist adventure

The Free Trader – a Young Adult Science Fiction Action Adventure

Cygnus Space Opera – A Young Adult Space Opera (set in the Free Trader universe)

Darklanding (co-written with Scott Moon) – a Space Western

Rick Banik – Spy & Terrorism Action Adventure

Become a Successful Indie Author – a non-fiction work

Enemy of my Enemy (co-written with Tim Marquitz) – a galactic alien military space opera

Superdreadnought (co-written with Tim Marquitz) – a military space opera

Metal Legion (co-written with Caleb Wachter) - a military space opera

End Days (co-written with E.E. Isherwood) – a post-apocalyptic adventure

Mystically Engineered (co-written with Valerie Emerson) – dragons in space (coming Jan 2019)

Monster Case Files (co-written with Kathryn Hearst) – a young-adult cozy mystery series (coming Mar 2019)

BOOKS BY MICHAEL ANDERLE

For a complete list of books by Michael Anderle, please visit:

www.lmbpn.com/ma-books/

All LMBPN Audiobooks are Available at Audible.com and iTunes

To see all LMBPN audiobooks, including those written by
Michael Anderle please visit:

www.lmbpn.com/audible

www.ingramcontent.com/pod-product-compliance
Lightning Source LLC
Chambersburg PA
CBHW050242110726
47898CB00007B/2240